"Sorry if I sounded like a dictator—"

But Gianna refused to be soothed by Blake's words. "I suppose you want me to give up my weekend because you intend to go on location with her!"

"We're paying her five thousand dollars a day modeling fees," Blake said reasonably. "I'd like us to get our money's worth."

Gianna pounced. "Dammit, Blake! I understand that you're head over heels in love with her. But that's no excuse for ignoring the business. All I want is—"

The intercom buzzer sounded, but Blake ignored it. He started walking toward Gianna, slowly. Very softly he asked, "Gianna, are you so very angry because you're jealous of the attention Meghan's getting?"

Gianna gave a sharp laugh. Her heart was pounding. *Stop there*, she pleaded silently. *I can't stand to have you feel sorry for me.*

Leigh Michaels likes writing romance fiction spiced with humor and a dash of suspense and adventure. She holds a degree in journalism and teaches creative writing in Iowa. She and her husband, a photographer, have two children but include in their family a dog-pound mutt who thinks he's human and a Siamese "aristo-cat," both of whom have appeared in her books. When asked if her husband and children have also been characterized, the author pleads the Fifth Amendment.

Don't miss any of our special offers. Write to us at the following address for information on our newest releases.

Harlequin Reader Service
901 Fuhrmann Blvd., P.O. Box 1397, Buffalo, NY 14240
Canadian address: P.O. Box 603,
Fort Erie, Ont. L2A 5X3

Strictly Business

Leigh Michaels

Harlequin Books

TORONTO • NEW YORK • LONDON
AMSTERDAM • PARIS • SYDNEY • HAMBURG
STOCKHOLM • ATHENS • TOKYO • MILAN

Original hardcover edition published in 1987
by Mills & Boon Limited

ISBN 0-373-02951-9

Harlequin Romance first edition December 1988
Second printing December 1988

CHAPTER ONE

THE ROSY glow of the bedside lamp left the corners of the room in shadow. Lacy ruffled curtains shut out the early winter darkness of the city below. Fat, fluffy pillows were piled high against the brass headboard of the big bed. A wicker basket full of dark red apples was balanced uncertainly on the peach-coloured satin coverlet, next to a glossy fashion magazine. The clock on the bedside table noted discreetly that it was precisely ten minutes past two.

The young woman in the bed hadn't noticed the time. She was absorbed in the contents of the leather portfolio that lay open across her pyjama-clad knees, which were drawn up under the satin coverlet.

'*Pink Champagne,*' Gianna West said aloud, testing the sound against the emptiness of the room. She shook her head and tried the next phrase on the list. '*Velvet Rose.*' She wrinkled her nose. 'Blake, what on earth's the matter with you?' she asked the empty room. 'We're supposed to be naming a new perfume here, not a cocktail lounge!'

There was no answer. She sighed. Blake was never around when she needed him, she thought owlishly. She scribbled a note to herself on the edge of the page, and went back to reading suggested titles for the new scent that Westway Cosmetics would be introducing soon. '*Never My Love*. No, that's too negative. *Dream of Yesterday*—— Good heavens, we want to sell this perfume to women who have a future! *Captive Passion*——' She wadded up the list and threw it at the foot of the bed in disgust.

'What a bunch of idiotic names!' she muttered irritably. 'Obviously I'm going to have to do it myself.'

Well, tomorrow would do as well for that, she decided, patting back a yawn. She reached for another red apple from the basket and sliced it into quarters with the silver fruit knife that Blake had given her last Christmas. The apple split with a satisfyingly juicy crack, and Gianna bit deeply into a section and reached for the fashion magazine. Now for a little pleasant relaxation, she thought, after the cares of business.

Not that she really minded work, though. She flipped through the magazine pages, thinking about Westway. The company had been her preoccupation—almost an obsession—for the last five years, since she had rushed to finish her Master's degree in business administration so she could plunge into the company where her father had left off. Nobody had expected her to stay with it. They had all thought she was too young to know what she wanted. Especially Blake.

Blake had joined Westway before her. His father and hers had been the founding partners. It was funny, she thought, that everyone had assumed that Blake would come into the business, but no one had expected that Gianna would want to.

Blake hadn't hurried through school—Blake never exactly hurried at anything, Gianna thought, but he always seemed to finish ahead of schedule. And since he was a couple of years older than she, he had been installed in the main office of Westway while she was still in college. He had concentrated on learning the business at first hand, taking everything slowly and conservatively, observing every detail.

She thought sometimes that Blake Whittaker was still watching her thoughtfully, waiting for the day when she would give it up. Not that he was anxious to be rid of her, Gianna qualified hastily. No, she and Blake had a rare working relationship. Seldom did partners fit so well together, one's strengths filling in where the other was lacking, and never arguing over anything . . .

Well, almost never, Gianna thought with a grin,

remembering a few times when the corporate structure of Westway had trembled under a quarrel. But usually, she and Blake were perfect partners, she overflowing with ideas, he the management genius who patiently fitted all the pieces together and made the innovations work. Yes, she thought, I'm a lucky woman, with the perfect job, the perfect partner.

Nothing else had ever captured Gianna's interest and devotion as the cosmetics industry had. Since she was a tiny girl, lipstick and perfume had been—not dress-up playthings as they were to other little girls, but the stuff of life.

She had tried other fields. Her father had insisted, despite her temper tantrums, that she give other things a try, and so Gianna had worked at various jobs during summers and after school. She had been horribly jealous of Blake, who had spent his summers at Westway.

She supposed, looking back, that her father had been wise. By the time she had finally joined the family corporation, Gianna knew with absolute certainty that it was the only thing she ever wanted to do. She had spent the last five years making up for lost time.

She turned the page, and Meghan stared up at her from the four-colour ad. Meghan, the model with the single name. Her face was quickly becoming the best-known in the world, with her true-green eyes, her black hair, the heart-shaped face with the perfect mouth, the classic nose.

'Now why couldn't nature have given me those sort of looks?' Gianna asked herself. She tugged at a lock of hair that had fallen over her shoulder. It was brown—not chestnut, nor almost auburn, nor the colour of dark honey, but merely brown. So were her eyes. Oh, they were nice enough, but certainly nothing unusual. Her face was an ordinary oval, with a nose that had a distinct tendency to tilt, and she was far too short to carry off the dramatic clothes her heart craved.

'Wouldn't you think,' she asked the room at large, 'that Nature could have done a better job? If I looked like Meghan, I could do a whole lot more for the image of the cosmetics industry!'

And the heck of it was, she added, that Meghan looked even better in person. The model had been part of a fashion show she and Blake had attended just weeks ago. It had been a rare appearance for Meghan; these days she seldom had enough time—and clients seldom had enough money—to make such limited personal engagements possible. It was the first time Gianna had ever seen the woman on the modelling ramp, and she had punched Blake in the ribs. 'That's Meghan!' she had whispered.

'I know.' He hadn't taken his eyes off the woman.

'What do you think of the dress?'

'I hate it,' he had said briefly. 'It's not your sort of thing at all; you aren't tall enough to carry it off. What I want to know is this—is the model for sale?' And for careful, think-it-over-before-acting Blake to react that way—yes, Meghan was really something . . .

Thoughtfully, Gianna stared down at Meghan's wide eyes on the magazine page. The woman breathed sexual excitement, she thought, even from the coldness of print. The unattainable—that was what Meghan stood for.

That was the quality she had sensed in this new perfume, Gianna thought. It was an unusual blend of scents, with a musk base—unlike anything she had ever smelled before. 'Too glamorous for me,' she muttered. 'I'm the all-American girl sort.' This new scent had left her with the impression that the wearer was not quite touchable, somehow . . .

That's it, she thought. She reached for the bedside telephone and punched a string of numbers. *Sensually Meghan*, she thought. That's what we'll call it, if we can only get her to do the ad campaign. It shouldn't be hard to persuade her——

'Hello, Gianna.' The voice that answered was slightly

husky, just a little rough around the edges.

She was momentarily diverted. 'How did you know it was me?'

There was a groan, and she could hear the rustle of sheets as Blake rolled over. 'Because nobody else calls me at two-thirty in the morning.'

'Is it that late? Gee, I'm sorry.'

'No, you're not.'

'Besides,' she said, 'if you weren't such a stick-in-the-mud someone else might call you now and then.'

Blake grunted. 'What is it this time?'

She was startled. 'You sound upset, Blake. Were you busy?'

'At this hour? What did you expect me to be doing?'

'Well, it is Saturday night. I suppose you might have——' she hesitated, and put it delicately, 'company.'

'As a matter of fact, I was sleeping. Alone.'

'Don't bite my head off! I only thought, since you're an eligible bachelor—well, I can always hope that some day you'll find the woman of your dreams.'

Blake sighed. 'And to answer your next question, I spent the evening having dinner with my parents.'

'What a waste, Blake! How do you ever expect to enjoy yourself if you throw away weekends like this?'

'Gianna, if I did have a woman in my bed at this moment I wouldn't tell you.'

'And why not?' she asked indignantly. 'As hard as I've tried to find you a suitable companion——'

'That's exactly why I wouldn't tell you. You'd expect a critique.'

'I always like to know how your dates turn out. When was the last time you had one, anyway?'

'Mind your own business, Gianna. Would you like it if I asked how your date went tonight?'

'Well, I wouldn't snap your head off if you did,' Gianna said reasonably. 'As a matter of fact, it was a disaster. He kept calling me Gina——'

'I'm sorry I brought it up,' muttered Blake.

'I told him that my name has three syllables. "It's Gee-ann-uh," I kept telling him, but——'

Blake sighed. 'Honey, what did you have on your little mind when you called? There must have been something.'

'Oh, there was, but now I can't remember. All this yelling at me drove it straight out of my head. Did you tell your parents Hi for me?'

'Yes. I gave them your love and told them how much you wished you could have been there, and if it only hadn't been for this important dinner at which you were the main speaker, wild horses couldn't have kept you away——'

'Let's not go overboard,' Gianna recommended. 'You didn't have to make excuses for me.'

'Oh, but I did. Mother would have been heartbroken if I'd told her you preferred a blind date to celebrating my birthday with me.'

'Oh.' It was a very small sound. 'I completely forgot it was your birthday.'

'I know.'

'Well, you should have told them it was business.'

'They wouldn't have believed it. If it had been business, I'd have been there with you.'

'Now I remember,' said Gianna. 'That's what I called you about. It was business. Remember Meghan?'

'Of course. Half the men in this country put themselves to sleep at night by dreaming about Meghan.'

'Do you really, Blake?' She was intrigued.

'I didn't say that.'

'You didn't? It certainly sounded like it. Well, at any rate, don't you think she'd make a good perfume ad? It would be a terrific boost for her career, too—to be associated with Westway. We could name it after her—the new fragrance, I mean.'

'You didn't like my list of names, hmm?'

'Really, Blake! Did you expect me to?'

'Come to think of it, no. You never do.' He yawned.

'Could we talk about this tomorrow, Gianna? Or better yet, Monday at the office?'

'What's wrong with right now?' she asked.

'It's the middle of the night.'

'That didn't keep you from telling me about your mother.'

'Gianna, so help me, I'm going to get an unlisted phone number!' groaned Blake.

'No, you won't. You know I'm at my most creative at this hour.'

'Unfortunately for me.'

'How are your parents, by the way?' she asked him.

'We'll discuss it in the morning, Gianna!'

'You don't need to yell,' she said primly. 'I can take a hint. Doughnuts and coffee at nine?'

'Your place or mine?'

'Yours, of course. I forgot to buy doughnuts when I stopped at the store today.' Gianna put the phone down, turned the light off, and settled back into her nest of pillows with a sigh.

Really, she thought, sometimes it almost seemed as if Blake wasn't interested in Westway at all!

It was precisely nine when she pulled the door of her own apartment closed behind her and walked briskly down the hall. It had been Blake's idea that she should move into the building where he already lived; he had said that if he was going to have to rescue her from blown fuses, dripping taps, and spoons stuck in waste disposals, he'd rather not have to drive clear across Chicago to do so. She had thought that he was going a bit overboard with the exaggeration. It had, after all, been only one blown fuse and a broken shower head in her old apartment, and she wouldn't have called Blake at all if her landlord hadn't refused to come over in the middle of the night. After all, as she had tried to explain to him, a non-functioning shower was an emergency as far as she was concerned.

'And the spoon down the waste disposal is plainly Blake's imagination,' she told herself firmly. She had never done that, and she didn't expect to. But he had been right about the apartment next to his being a nice one, and so, six months ago, she had moved.

There was no answer when she tapped on the door, and the Sunday newspaper lay undisturbed on the mat. 'Lazybones,' she muttered, and rummaged through her pockets for her key. There was no sign of life when she stepped into the apartment, so she went straight to the kitchen and started the coffee. She read the newspaper while she waited for it to perk, and as soon as the pot finished its cycle, she poured two mugs full and carried them back to Blake's bedroom.

He was sprawled across the bed, his cheek nestled against a pillow swathed in a leopardskin print. Gianna noted the pattern with approval; she'd given him the set last Christmas, and told him that every bachelor should own something of the sort. But frankly, she decided, until now she hadn't believed that he even appreciated the gesture.

He was awfully nice-looking, she decided, even with the dark morning stubble of beard and his black hair standing on end. He was tall and broad-shouldered, and even tailored clothes didn't completely hide his well-developed muscles. This morning, the sheet had slipped, and the muscles in his arms and back were apparent, even relaxed as he was in sleep, because he wasn't wearing a pyjama jacket.

Gianna shook her head. I don't understand why some woman hasn't snapped him up, she thought. He's really a very decent sort of guy.

She waved the mug under his nose and set it on the table, then curled up at the foot of the bed. 'Good morning, Blake,' she said cheerfully.

His nose twitched. He frowned just a little, then opened one eye warily, looked at her, and groaned. 'It's too early,' he muttered.

'I couldn't find the doughnuts. Did you hide them somewhere?'

'I forgot them, too.'

Gianna sipped her coffee. 'Well, you could have told me that last night, she complained. 'Then I wouldn't have bothered to get up so early.'

'I couldn't have been so lucky.' He pulled the pillows around and propped himself up. 'To what do I owe the honour of finding you in my bedroom?'

'Well, there was no answer when I knocked, so I came on in.' She noted, with amazement, that a slight flush had crept into his cheeks. 'You're embarrassed!' she exclaimed with delight.

'It is a little unusual,' Blake pointed out.

'But not exactly abnormal, for heaven's sake. You are a man, you know. It's not unheard-of for you to have a woman in your bedroom.'

'That's not the point.'

'Oh, I know,' Gianna said wisely. 'You mean you're not wearing any pyjamas, and you'd like me to clear out while you get dressed. That's all right. I've seen you without clothes before—remember, we used to take baths together.'

'That was when you were two and I was four,' Blake said drily.

'Picky, picky! If you're asking me to leave——'

'I am. You can go down to the corner and get the doughnuts while I take a shower.'

'I thought I'd take you out to lunch for your birthday. We can talk about Meghan.'

'I don't want to spend Sunday discussing perfume. You talk about my lack of social life, but the only thing you ever think about is Westway.'

Gianna put her nose in the air. 'Well, at least I have a social life.'

'Right. With a guy who can't even pronounce your name.' He tugged the top sheet out from under her and wrapped it toga-style around his waist.

'If he was the only one, I'd be worried,' Gianna admitted. 'But there are hundreds of men out there just waiting for me to notice them——'

'I know,' Blake said unkindly. 'You've told me.' The bathroom door shut firmly behind him.

'I'm really worried about you,' she called. 'You've turned thirty now, and if you don't get married soon there won't be any eligible women left!'

He didn't answer. The only sound was the hiss of the shower spray.

Gianna mentioned it again, at lunch. They had their favourite corner table at Coq au Vin, where the Sunday champagne brunch was the best in town. Gianna sipped her champagne, stifled a sneeze as the bubbles tickled her throat, and said, 'Blake, don't you *ever* think about getting married?'

He groaned. 'Don't start, Gianna! Isn't it enough that my mother nags me about it?'

'See?' she said with satisfaction. 'I knew I wasn't the only one who thought that way.'

'It isn't fair,' he sighed. 'Nobody ever says anything to you about getting married. You're twenty-eight—I'd think they'd be concerned about you becoming an old maid.'

'I'm in the prime of life,' Gianna announced grandly. 'This isn't the Dark Ages, you know. A woman doesn't have to be married at all.' She giggled. 'Besides, I told my mother years ago that if she ever started hinting about sons-in-law or grandchildren, I'd never speak to her again. She's never dared to mention the subject.'

'Thanks for the advice. I'll try it.'

'It wouldn't work for you,' she told him. 'Your mother knows what a softie you are. Besides, she's right.'

'Why are you so anxious to get me married off, Gianna?'

She shrugged. 'I'm not, actually. As far as I'm concerned, you wouldn't even have to go through with the vows and all. I just think you'd be happier with a little female companionship.'

Blake shrugged and refilled her champagne glass. 'What could be more companionable than finding you in my bedroom on Sunday morning?'

'Having someone there on Saturday night,' Gianna replied promptly. 'Your mother is a pretty shrewd woman. I'm sure she has some ideas about who you ought to marry.'

He sighed. 'Gianna, how would you like to talk about your brilliant idea concerning Meghan and the perfume?'

'I thought you said you didn't want to talk about business on Sunday.'

'I'll make an exception for you.'

'Oh.' She plunged into a recital of her idea, the ad campaign possibilities, the promotional value. 'It will cost us, of course,' she finished up. 'Meghan's name is worth a lot right now. But it would also be valuable to her to be identified with Westway. There would have to be personal appearances, and things like that——'

He was frowning, and she paused. Despite the fact that Gianna occasionally referred to Blake in the heat of a dispute as 'stodgy', she had nothing but respect for his opinion. If he didn't think an idea would fly, chances were that he was right. She had learned that the hard way, in her first year in the company, when on several occasions she had pushed past his objections and fallen flat on her face.

But this time, Blake merely drew idle patterns on the linen tablecloth with the handle of his spoon, then said, 'I don't know why it wouldn't work, if she isn't tied up with a competing project. But don't commit yourself, Gianna. We'd have to do a bit of investigating first. We wouldn't want to find out after we'd invested a million in advertising that Meghan isn't really the upstanding citizen we want identified with Westway.'

'Actually,' Gianna said confidentially, 'I thought perhaps you'd call her up. As a man, you'll get further.'

Blake raised an eyebrow. 'So you do think I'm good for something?'

'You have wonderful instincts, darling.'

'I don't even know her last name.'

'Neither does anyone else, Blake. It's part of the mysterious aura. You'll find her; I have confidence in you.'

'She may not even want to talk to me.'

Gianna leaned across the table and patted his hand. 'That's your biggest problem when it comes to women, Blake,' she said. 'You lack confidence.'

'I wish you'd stop treating me like a mildly retarded adolescent,' Blake complained. 'I do have my share of feminine companionship, you know.'

'It's probably my fault,' she murmured. 'I make things too easy for you.'

Blake choked on his champagne.

Gianna glared at him. 'I'm serious,' she announced. 'I'm always there. It discourages you from getting a date, because you know you can always take me. Last month when we went to the opera, for example. Really, Blake—you called me just two hours before curtain time——'

'What you don't know,' he said mildly, 'is that I'd already exhausted my little black book by then. Nobody wanted to go to the opera that night.'

'Not on two hours' notice, no.'

'I'd spent days on the phone,' he said, looking mournful. 'And actually, I only waited so long to call you because I knew if I asked you any earlier, you'd forget all about it.'

'That's got nothing to do with it. We're going to have to work at this.' She stared thoughtfully across the table at him. 'Perhaps we just need to find some new entries for your black book. I know plenty of——'

'I think I can manage that by myself, Gianna.' Blake's words were soft, but his tone was suddenly not to be argued with.

Gianna, however, hadn't noticed. She was waving

across the room at a redhead who had just come in. 'There's Cluny Brown,' she said to Blake. He looked unmoved.

The woman swooped across the room and vigorously kissed the air beside Gianna's cheek. 'It's so nice to see you,' she said. Her eyes were on Blake, who rose politely.

Gianna lifted an eyebrow. So Cluny Brown reacted to Blake like steel filings to a magnet, hmm? Well, he was good-looking. She glanced at the young man who was following Cluny, carrying her fur jacket. It wasn't cold enough yet for fur, Gianna thought, but that was Cluny all over. Not a bad-looking man, either. He looked a little dippy about Cluny.

Then he looked at Gianna, and she decided that perhaps she'd been mistaken about his feelings for Cluny. Gianna had got positive responses from men before, but this was the first time she had ever been actively adored, she thought drily. The young man bore a remarkable resemblance to a beagle puppy!

'And who is this?' she asked, and offered her hand.

'I'm Norman Brown, ma'am,' he said, and took her fingers as carefully as if they were made of antique glass.

'My third cousin, from Houston,' offered Cluny. She was still staring soulfully up at Blake.

'Are you going to be here long?' asked Gianna.

'Not nearly long enough,' he said, with a touch of Texas twang. 'Now that I've met you.' Then he blushed beet-red, as if he had said something impolite.

Gianna sighed. 'Well, we'll have to help Cluny show you the town,' she said. 'Dinner next Saturday night? Blake's been wanting to spend some more time with Cluny. It will give us a chance to get better acquainted, Norman.'

Blake glared across the table at her. Norman looked as if his favourite fantasy had suddenly sprung to life. Cluny was clinging to Blake's arm. 'What a lovely idea!' she crooned. 'There's that new restaurant up on Rush

Street—I've been wanting to go. What a special idea, Blake!'

Ah, well, thought Gianna, I didn't want any recognition for the idea. Let Blake get the credit. She looked up at Norman, who was still clutching her hand, and sighed inwardly. It would be worth putting up with an evening in his company, she thought, if Blake had a good time. And Cluny would make sure of that.

Cluny and Norman went off to their table, and Blake, looking like a thundercloud, sat down, folded his arms on the edge of the table, and glared at Gianna.

'What's your problem?' she asked.

'I was just wondering,' murmured Blake, 'whether the pleasure of murdering you right here would make up for the inconvenience of spending the rest of my life in jail. On the whole, I think it would.'

'What? I don't understand you, Blake. Do you mean the thing with Cluny?'

'Of course I mean the thing with Cluny. What other outrageous stunts have you pulled this morning? I do not want to spend Saturday night——'

'You can't mean you have something better to do? Besides, Cluny is a nice girl. She's always ready for a good time. She might even be the sort who'll go to the opera on two hours' notice.'

'I have one woman like that in my life,' Blake pointed out. 'I have no need of another. Let's go.'

'Well, I was only trying to pep up your social life. You could at least be a good sport about it.'

He retrieved her wool coat from the cloakroom attendant and held it for her. 'I'll be a good sport on Saturday night,' he said, 'since it appears that I have no choice in the matter. But in the meantime, please don't get the impression that I approve. And if you try anything like this again——'

The air was cold against her face as they walked across the parking lot to his car. She slipped on a patch of hard-packed snow. 'It's awfully slippery out here, isn't it?

Wouldn't you think they'd at least clear the concrete off?'

Blake cast a scathing glance at her high-heeled pumps. 'Some sensible shoes would help,' he said. 'And stop trying to change the subject!'

She settled herself in the passenger seat and said plaintively, 'Goodness, Blake, one would think I'd asked the girl to marry you!'

'I wouldn't put it past you!'

Gianna blinked. She had never heard quite that note in Blake's voice before.

'I'm sorry, dear,' she said soothingly. 'I only have your best interests at heart, you know.'

'You and my mother,' grumbled Blake.

She snapped her fingers. 'Now that's an idea,' she said. 'I haven't had lunch with your mother in ages. Perhaps I'll call her up this week.'

'I wouldn't advise that you ask my mother her opinion on whom I should marry.' The car accelerated hard and slipped neatly into traffic, pressing Gianna back into the leather seat.

'Oh? Why not? I'm sure she has an opinion. Your mother is really a wonderful judge of character. Perhaps you should take Cluny out to meet her——'

'I wouldn't take Cluny anywhere, if I wasn't pushed into it.'

'Now, Blake! How do you expect to recognise the woman of your dreams if you won't spend any time with women in general?'

'Why are you so certain I'm looking for the woman of my dreams?' he asked drily.

'My goodness, we're touchy this morning!' She settled herself primly. 'Yes, I think I'll have a chat with your mother.'

'I wouldn't, Gianna.' He swung the car into his numbered spot in the parking ramp under the apartment building.

'Why on earth not? She's obviously got to stop nagging you or you'll be turned off the idea completely.'

He didn't look at her, but she noticed that his hand was clenched on the wheel.

'Your mother and I get along beautifully,' she went on. 'I'm sure I can talk to her about it.'

'That's part of the problem,' murmured Blake.

'What? That we both care very much for you?'

'That's the other part of the problem. You see, Gianna my dear, my mother thinks——' He stopped.

Gianna slid out of the car without waiting for him to open her door. 'Yes?' she asked, trying to keep up with his long strides on the way to the elevator.

He looked down at her, and there was sternly repressed humour in his eyes. 'I ought to just let you walk into it,' he mused. 'You deserve every uncomfortable moment of it.' Then he sighed, as if thinking better of it, and said, very clearly, 'You see, Gianna, my mother thinks I should marry you.'

CHAPTER TWO

GIANNA stifled a giggle. 'You're joking, aren't you?'

'There's no joke about it.'

'Oh.' She walked across the lobby at his side, in silence. 'That's a ridiculous idea, Blake. You did tell her that, didn't you?'

He looked down at her, a quizzical gleam in his eyes.

'Well, it is,' she went on. 'We're best friends, for heaven's sake! Gwen is carrying things a little far if she thinks it means we could ever be serious about each other!'

'Let's just say,' drawled Blake, 'that Mother doesn't think it's ridiculous.'

'I see. Well, what are you going to do about it?'

He was startled. 'Nothing. Why should I waste my time over it?'

'But she's got to be disillusioned, Blake. That sort of thing can't go on.'

'Why not? It's been going on for years—apparently it was the topic under discussion clear back when your mother and mine were giving us baths in the same tub.'

'My mother, too?' squeaked Giana. 'You'll never make me believe my mother would take part in any such thing!'

'Well, she did,' Blake said unsympathetically. 'Obviously you didn't stop them from making plans when you issued your grandiose threat. They just stopped talking to you about it. And I'm not going to be the one who tries to blast the idea out of their heads.'

'Then I will. It's simply got to stop.'

'Be my guest.' He stopped at her door. 'Do you want to play gin rummy this afternoon?'

Gianna shook her head. 'I'd love to,' she said. 'But I've been putting my laundry off all week.'

'Bring it down,' said Blake. 'I've told you to use the washer and drier any time you like.'

'I know, but I hate to bother you.'

He said mildly, 'I don't know why you'd draw the line there.'

She stuck her tongue out at him, much as she had been accustomed to do in childhood. 'You're being sarcastic, and it isn't fair,' she announced.

'So go to the laundromat,' he shrugged. 'See if I care.'

She turned the key in her door, then smiled suddenly. 'You care,' she accused. 'You can't play gin without me, that's why.'

'At least I appreciate your brain. All young Norman what's-his-name saw was your body.'

'Do you think that's what attracted him?' Gianna, diverted, glanced at her reflection in the mirror-lined hallway.

'Well, he did only see you sitting down,' Blake said. 'That might have influenced his judgement.'

'That's what I love about you,' she grinned. 'You never let me get big-headed.'

'I'll send a bill for my services. Are you playing gin or not?'

'I am.'

'Good. I'll go start stacking the cards while you gather the dirty clothes.'

Gianna got in the final shot. 'I don't mind,' she said. 'You stacking the cards, that is. I know it's the only way you stand a chance of winning.'

She closed the door on him and went to change her clothes. It was rather nice to have attracted that boy's attention at first glance, she thought. At twenty-eight, it was flattering to know that men occasionally found her striking. Gianna had long ago concluded that, though she wasn't bad-looking, she was hardly the type that men swooned over in droves. She was wholesome-looking, Blake had told her once. She wrinkled her nose at the memory.

She had her share of men friends, and here and there one who seemed to be serious about her. Some day, she was convinced, she would find the right man to fall in love with. In the mean time, she was in no hurry. For one thing, she wasn't sure she wanted to try balancing marriage and career. She'd seen a lot of young women fail when they tried to combine the two. Either the job or the marriage suffered when a woman tried to do too much.

Not that she was exactly desperate, she told herself. Some day, the right man—one who would understand what the company meant to her—would come along. In the meantime, Westway would keep her occupied.

She changed her peach-coloured suit for jeans and an old, battered tomato-red sweater, and piled the clothes to be laundered into a basket. It was decent of Blake to offer the use of his washer and drier, she thought; he'd put them in just weeks ago because he was tired of sitting in the laundry room and waiting for a machine to be free. Blake was always so practical, Gianna thought. He always saw things clearly, and knew exactly how to go about persuading people and things to co-operate.

That was why she hoped that he would call Meghan this week about the perfume line. It might be just the boost that Westway needed just now.

Blake had left the door of his apartment open. She carried her basket to the kitchen and started sorting clothes. 'Can you imagine Cluny's face if she saw this room right now?' she giggled as Blake came in. 'Lacy underthings strewn all over your kitchen—Blake, you look like a libertine!'

'Must we talk about Cluny?' he sighed.

'You don't want to? Can I borrow some detergent?'

'You can't borrow detergent, Gianna. You can't

borrow anything that's consumed, because it can't be returned.' He reached for a box on a top shelf. 'But you may have as much as you need.'

'Thanks. I forgot to pick some up in the store yesterday.'

'Did you remember anything?' he asked drily.

She paused. 'I got plenty of apples.'

'You know, he said thoughtfully, 'perhaps Mother's idea isn't so far off track, anyway.'

'What's that supposed to mean?' she demanded.

'Well, I'm doing all your shopping anyway. I might as well marry you.'

'Funny—very funny! Deal the cards; I'll be right there.'

Blake's apartment was larger than Gianna's. Where her kitchen was scarcely big enough for two people to stand, his had room for a small table and a couple of chairs. It had even included a long narrow closet, which now held the appliances. Blake believed in having all the comforts of home, she thought.

Sometimes, she reflected with a twinge of sadness, she missed the big house she had grown up in. But that was gone now, and there was no sense in regretting it. It would have been far too large for her to live in alone, anyway. The only time the extra rooms would have been used at all was when her parents came back to visit.

When her father had retired from Westway because of ill health, his doctor had recommended a milder climate. So John and Carol West had sold their house and bought an apartment in Florida. Whenever they came back to Illinois, they stayed with Gwen and Hal Whittaker— Blake's parents—in their big house in Oak Park, just blocks away from where Gianna had grown up.

Blake was right about one thing, though, she reflected. The Wests and the Whittakers had always been close— even close enough, perhaps, that they might have joked about their offspring marrying. But it would have been only a joke, she thought.

'Sometimes I wish I'd bought the house from Mom and Dad,' she said.

Blake looked up from his cards. 'What brings that up?'

'Oh, just sitting here. Your apartment looks so homey. Mine is only a place to live.'

He smiled. 'I had a good decorator.'

'I did have some good ideas, didn't I?' she said modestly.

He nodded. 'Of course, if you'd spend even half as many hours on your place as you did telling me what to do here——'

She made a face at him. 'I haven't had time, and you know it. When you moved here, I was still living at home, and it was like playing house to come over here and plan things out. Now it's a little different.'

'What makes you think having a house would make it easier?'

'It wouldn't. You're right, of course.' She sighed. 'Why do you always have to be right, Blake?'

'Gin.' He put the cards down with a flourish. 'I must admit I'm glad you didn't talk John into giving you the house.'

'Why? And I said I would have bought it, anyway— even if he'd tried to give it to me.'

He ignored the comment. 'Because I could have spent my life dealing with falling plaster, bats, and draughty windows, that's why.'

'There was only one bat in the twenty years we lived there,' Gianna pointed out.

'And I got the honour of rescuing you from it.'

'It wasn't my fault that my parents were gone.' She counted the cards left in her hand. 'I've got sixteen points.'

'Aha!' He wrote his score down. 'Are we playing for the usual stakes?'

'Why do you wait until you're winning before you discuss the bet?'

'I just wondered how hard I should try.'

'Something tells me I'm going to get stuck with the bill for the pizza tonight,' Gianna said drily.

'Only if you don't pay attention to your cards. Half my gin came from your discards. What caused this obsession with the house, anyway?'

'I was just thinking about Christmas coming up. I always miss the celebrations we used to have.'

Blake shrugged. 'We were little kids, then. You can't expect it to be the same now.'

'Did you ever regret being an "only", Blake?' she asked.

He grinned. 'Of course not. You were always tagging along behind me. I didn't realise you weren't my sister till I was thirteen.'

Gianna made a face at him. There had been a sad note in her voice, but it disappeared as she challenged, 'Some of us are slower than others at comprehending the facts of life.'

'That's the sharpest thing you've said all day.'

It was odd, Gianna thought, but Blake sounded almost serious. Well, that couldn't be allowed to go on. 'You know, Blake, if you weren't so awfully good at fixing things like leaky taps, nobody would ask you to do it. I'll have to tell Cluny what a peach you are.'

'Oh, I see we're out for blood today. Tell you what, I'll buy the pizza if you'll leave Cluny out of the conversation.'

After that, the game of gin rummy became a war that was interrupted periodically whenever Gianna got up to move the newly clean clothes from washer to drier. When she reached the last load, she looked up from a pile of tailored blouses and offered, 'If you have some dirty shirts I'll do them for you.'

'How generous,' mocked Blake. 'I only have to supply the washer, drier, water, and detergent.'

'Blake, you sound like an accountant!' she called after him as he went off to rummage in his closet.

Darkness was closing down about the high-rise apartment complex, and the city lights were starting to gleam gold along the Magnificent Mile. The long windows of Blake's living-room faced towards the turbulent shore of Lake Michigan. It made Gianna cold just to watch the rolling waves, whipping into whitecaps as they smashed against the shoreline. The calendar said that the first day of winter was still three weeks off, but the lake said differently. Gianna shivered and went to call the pizza delivery service.

The telephone rang under her hand, and she picked it up. 'Whittaker residence,' she said brightly.

'Hello, Gianna.'

'Mom! How did you know where to find me?'

'I'd tried your place several times. It seemed only reasonable to ask Blake what had become of you.'

Why? Gianna wondered uneasily. Then she told herself sharply to stop being silly. If it hadn't been for that nonsense Blake was talking earlier, about his mother's plans for them, it would never have occurred to her to be suspicious of her own parent! After all, Gwen Whittaker sometimes called Gianna when she was looking for Blake . . . Best friends usually have an idea of what the other one is doing, Gianna thought crossly. It doesn't mean any more than that.

'Gianna? I just wanted to tell you that since you've decided not to come to Florida for the holidays——'

'I'm really sorry about it, Mom,' Gianna interrupted breathlessly. 'I just can't see how I can take a week off then.'

'Gianna dear, if you'll let me finish my sentence—John and I called the Whittakers and cadged an invitation. We're coming to Chicago for Christmas.'

'Oh, good! But are you sure Daddy won't mind the weather?'

'He'll be fine. We're both looking forward to snow for Christmas, for a change.'

'The holidays don't seem quite the same without it, do they?'

Carol West sounded anxious. 'Will you be able to come later in the winter, dear?'

'Probably. I could at least squeeze out a long weekend, I'm sure.'

Blake came into the room in time to hear the last few words. 'Don't get any ideas,' he ordered. 'If you're making plans for next weekend——'

She waved a hand at him for quiet.

'What was that? It sounded like a wounded bear,' Carol said curiously.

'Oh, that was only Blake, being his usual charming self. We've got a double date next weekend, and he's so delighted he can't keep it to himself.'

There was a gurgle of laughter. 'I can guess! Give him my sympathy.'

'I will,' promised Gianna.'

'And tell him that if he wants to have your full attention, he should learn to plan ahead and leave the other couple out of it.'

Gianna blinked in astonishment, but before she had gathered the words to correct her mother's mistaken impression, Carol West had skipped blithely to another topic. It was nearly twenty minutes later when Gianna put the phone down.

'Well?' asked Blake. 'Was that for me?'

'No.' Gianna was still wavering with the shock. 'My mother seems to think we're dating—you and me.'

'See? I told you she was in on it.'

'We've never dated. Where they ever got the idea——'

'We do go places together a lot,' he pointed out.

'So do all kinds of friends. Blake, there's never been anything romantic between us. Where those people got the idea is beyond me.'

'Wishful thinking,' Blake said promptly. 'And not worth fussing about. You're down a grand total of six hundred points, and you owe me a pizza.'

'Oh. Now I remember what I was going to do.' Gianna started to dial the number of the pizza palace, and broke off. 'Just throw those shirts in the washer, would you? And there are half a dozen blouses over there, too.'

'I don't believe this,' said Blake. 'Why is it that every time you start out to do me a favour, I end up doing the work?'

'It's part of what you love about me,' Gianna said lightly. She was trying to decide which toppings to put on the pizza, so she didn't see Blake's face. If she had, she might have wondered why he looked so thoughtful.

The corporate office of Westway Cosmetics was part of one of the manufacturing plants, which sprawled across acres of expensive real estate in one of Chicago's north-western suburbs. It was a long way from the lake-front high-rise, and as Gianna manoeuvred her little car through the morning rush hour traffic on that Friday morning, she regretted even more deeply that the house she had grown up in had been sold. It and the Whittakers' home were just a few miles from the plant.

'I could sleep an hour later in the morning and still make it to work on time,' she reflected.

She had once accused her father of building this plant to suit his own convenience, and not because it was the best location. He had laughed, but he hadn't disputed her conclusion.

But she had to admit that there were advantages to living on the lake-front, too. 'And some day,' she told herself as her car came to an abrupt stop in a traffic-jammed intersection, 'I might even think of one or two.'

But the jam broke up eventually, and with her good humour restored, Gianna drove on towards the plant. It was nice to be within walking distance of the shops along the Magnificent Mile, she decided. And it was pleasant to be near the museums, the concert hall, and the theatres.

A low sign near the street stated the corporation's name, giving no clue to what Westway's business was. Only the pair of intertwined initials—one a gold W, the other medium blue—gave a hint. Those initials, which formed Westway's trademark, also appeared on every lipstick case and eye-shadow compact that the company produced. One of the initials stood for West, the other for Whittaker. I wonder, Gianna thought, which is which.

Blake's car was already in his reserved spot. That wasn't unusual, she thought. Blake was never late. She grabbed the leather portfolio and the brightly wrapped box from the back seat of her car and started for the office door, gasping as a sudden cold wind lifted the hem of her skirt.

Despite the dull greyness of the outdoors, the office was warm, sunny, and bright. Good lighting always made ePeryone feel better, Gianna knew. It certainly worked on her this morning. Who needs a vacation in Florida, she thought, when you have central heating?

At any rate, she decided, she might as well think that way, since she was stuck in Chicago's cold for the next couple of months.

Her own office was a warm haven. She drew the curtains across the long windows that looked out over the car park and settled herself at the desk to sort out the contents of the portfolio. She had worked late last night on a marketing strategy for the new perfume, and she was anxious to show it to Blake. She reached behind her chair and rapped three times on the wall that separated her office from his.

Jungle intercom, they called it. Over the years, it had developed into a code. Three knocks meant, 'I need to see you.' Two said, 'I'll be right over.' One stood for, 'Come to see me, please.' Once in a while, Blake resorted to Morse code to make his point; it usually accomplished the purpose, because Gianna could never tell a dot from a dash; she had to go flying next door to see what he meant.

This time, one rap resounded through the wall. Gianna sighed and picked up the portfolio. 'Wouldn't you think he could come over instead of making me carry all of this stuff around?' she asked the empty room.

Their secretary had, when she first came to work for them, looked horrified when they dashed in and out of each other's offices without ever knocking on a door—and without ever interrupting an important call or conference. They had never told her about the jungle intercom. The rumour was that the two of them could read minds. Blake and Gianna had never troubled to correct it; sometimes it was a useful tool.

And sometimes, Gianna thought, it seemed more real than rumour, too. But that was easily explained. When two people worked as closely together as she and Blake had for the last five years, there wasn't anything important that they didn't know about one another.

The secretary stopped her at the door. 'He's on the telephone——'

'I know,' Gianna said briskly. 'He'll be off in a minute.'

The secretary looked confused, but she didn't argue. 'Mrs Whittaker called for you,' she added. 'She wondered if you'd like to come over for lunch today.'

What does Gwen want? Gianna wondered. Well, she'd told Blake she would talk to his mother about his crazy notion of hers; there was no point in putting if off.

'Call her back, please, and tell her I'd love to,' she said. 'I can make it by one o'clock.'

Blake was just putting the telephone down when she opened the door. He waved her to a chair and jotted a series of notes on a legal pad. The words marched precisely, in neat rows, down the page. If he didn't look at it again for five years, it would still be apparent what the conversation had covered.

Gianna settled herself in the leather chair beside his desk and tapped her eraser against her notes. She was anxious to see what he thought of this new strategy. Westway was doing good solid business, but some of the gloss had gone out of company profits last year. A new line, effectively marketed, could make all the difference in the world.

Blake pushed the notepad aside. 'What's that?' he asked, gesturing at the brightly wrapped package she had brought in.

'Just a late birthday present.' Gianna handed it across the desk. 'Though really, people who have birthdays this close to Christmas don't deserve gifts at all. Who were you talking to?'

'Meghan's manager.' It was absent-minded; Blake was pulling tape loose from the foil paper.

'Really? What did he say?'

'That he'll have to talk to Meghan, and that it would need the approval of her agency.'

'But did he sound interested?'

'I'd say so. We're to meet them for a drink and discuss the project.'

Gianna jumped out of her chair and threw her arms around him, almost upsetting his chair. 'I knew you could do it!' she exclaimed. 'Oh, Blake, isn't it wonderful?'

'Gianna, if you could control yourself——' He grabbed for the edge of the desk to keep his balance, and the package slid on to the floor.

She planted a kiss on his cheek. 'You're wonderful, Blake!'

'I haven't worked any miracles yet,' he warned. 'They've only agreed to talk about it.'

'When? As soon as possible, I hope; we really need to get this marketing campaign started. It should have been started months ago, when the chemists first hit on the formula.' The scent of his aftershave tickled her nose, and she realised suddenly that she still had her arms around him. She primly pulled away, picked up the package, and handed it to him.

'Next week.'

Gianna was instantly downcast. 'Not till then?'

'She's not even in town at the moment, Gianna. She'll be flying in next week to do a magazine layout.'

'Oh.' She retreated to her chair. 'Well, if that's the best we can do——'

Blake gave her a lopsided smile. 'One minute I'm a hero, the next—ah well, Gianna, that's life. But I assure you, I've been trying all week just to find the woman.'

Another week lost, she was thinking. But Blake was right; it wasn't just everyone who could intrigue Meghan's manager enough to get this far. She focused on the package in Blake's hands. 'For heaven's sake,' she said irritably, 'don't you know how to rip a package open? Do get into the spirit of it, Blake!'

'I'm always afraid you've wrapped up something that's going to jump out at me if I handle it carelessly. A kitten, or something.'

'If I'd known you wanted a cat——'

'That isn't what I said at all, Gianna.' He pulled the paper back from the box. 'But I wouldn't put it past you.'

'You're very difficult to buy presents for, you know,' she told him. 'Whatever you want, you go and get.'

'I wish I could,' Blake murmured. He lifted a record album out of the box. It was an obscure bit of classical music, an out-of-print album that had set her back a small fortune.

'Now you won't have to borrow my copy any more,' Gianna pointed out.

He grinned. 'My mother would say there's an easier way,' he said. 'If we'd get married, we wouldn't need two of everything.'

She made a face at him. 'I suppose you think that's funny. I'm having lunch with her today, by the way.'

'Well, be a little cautious about what you say, Gianna.'

'I intend to make everything perfectly clear. I don't think she'll be pestering you about the subject any more. Now, about the marketing strategy for the perfume, Blake——'

She was five minutes late and out of breath when she tapped on the door of Gwen Whittaker's all-white kitchen. Gwen herself answered it. 'Come in, dear,' she said. 'I'm so glad you could come today. We just don't have a chance to talk any more, it seems.'

And just what was it that Gwen wanted to talk about? Gianna wondered. She was even more uneasy when Gwen took her into the formal living-room, where a silver tray on a polished table held two stemmed crystal glasses and a decanter.

'Why so formal?' she asked, trying to keep her tone light. She was used to being entertained in Gwen's kitchen, with a mug of coffee.

Gwen shrugged. 'I just thought it would be nice for a change. I so seldom entertain any more that we've almost forgotten our manners.'

'If I'd known, I'd have made a grand entrance at the front door.'

Gwen smiled. 'I got out a bottle of sparkling cider—since I know you and Blake never drink anything stronger while you're working.'

'Blake?' Gianna echoed weakly. 'Is he coming to lunch, as well?'

'Heavens, no! Just us girls. Hal's playing racquetball at the club this morning, and he'll probably get into a poker game that will last all afternoon.' There was a pause, so tiny that it was hardly noticeable.

Gianna sipped the tart cider. Why, she wondered, did she have the feeling that Gwen was inviting her to confide something?

But Gwen was too good a hostess to allow a gap in

conversation. 'I hope you'll join us for Christmas,' she said. 'Come and stay for a few days, I mean. With John and Carol home, it will be like the old-fashioned holidays we used to have.'

That was a safe enough topic, Gianna thought. 'They were such nice holidays,' she murmured. 'And taking turns every year so that we spent Christmas Eve at one house and had dinner the next day at the other—I always thought that was a good idea.'

Gwen laughed. 'Except for the years when you and Blake were teenagers and couldn't abide each other,' she said. 'Then we wondered how wise it was! But mostly, it was wonderful. Everyone needs a big family on holidays.' For a moment, she sounded almost sad.

'We've always been a family, really,' Gianna said. 'The Wests and the Whittakers.'

'I know. I think it's marvellous, Gianna.' Gwen's smile was warm, madonna-like. 'Perhaps we should have our lunch now, don't you think?'

She led the way to the dining-room. I feel as if I'm being set up for something, Gianna thought. But she meekly took the seat beside Gwen and sampled the clear soup that her hostess ladled from a china tureen.

'I miss Carol so much,' said Gwen. 'We used to do everything together. It was unusual, really, that we all got along so well.'

'It will be nice to have them home for a while.'

'I hope you don't mind that they're staying here, instead of with you.'

'Where would I put them? Do you know, Gwen, I miss the old house sometimes.'

'I'm sure you do,' Gwen agreed.

'I even drove past it on the way over here,' Gianna admitted. 'That's why I was late.'

'It's for sale, you know.'

'Are you certain?'

Gwen frowned. 'Now who was it who told me that?

I'm sure that's the one, though.'

'There was no sign,' said Gianna.

'There wouldn't be. For Sale signs are forbidden in this neighbourhood. The estate agents don't like it when people try to make their own deals. Are you finished with your soup? I'll get the casserole.'

Gianna stared out of the window, across the broad, tree-lined street. Her old home up for sale? Was it only coincidence that this very morning she had been thinking about how convenient it would be to live closer to the plant?

Gwen came back with two plates, each holding a perfect puff pastry and a crisp green salad.

'You're a delightful cook,' Gianna told her as she lifted a flaky layer of the pastry with her fork.

'Oh, it's simple, really. I've had all my life to practise, and two men to feed for most of it.'

It reminded Gianna of what she had really come here to say. She sampled the casserole filling—chicken and vegetables and cheese, spiced just right—and said carefully, 'Blake mentioned that you'd said something about——' She stopped, and swallowed hard. This was much more difficult than she had expected.

She had always been able to talk to Gwen. In her teenage years, when she hadn't wanted to talk to her own mother, she had often tried her ideas out on Gwen, practising what she was going to tell Carol. This shouldn't be any harder, she scolded herself. All you're doing, after all, is telling the woman that you're not interested in marrying her son. Anyone with a grain of common sense could see that without being told.

And that was where the difficulty arose, she decided.

'Gwen,' she started again, 'Blake seems to think that you and Mom believe we'd be ideally suited to——'

'To what, dear?' Gwen was patiently interested; she was not, as Gianna had expected, flustered or upset.

'To be married. To each other,' Gianna finished, in a rush.

'Oh. How charming of him.'

Gianna released the breath she'd been holding, very slowly. 'Just what does that mean, Gwen?' she asked finally.

'Well, really, dear, it sounds just a bit like a fairytale when you put it that way.'

Gianna giggled in relief. How incredibly down-to-earth Gwen Whittaker was! 'It does, a bit, doesn't it?'

'Of course, darling. Happily-ever-after and all that stuff.'

I knew Blake couldn't be right, Gianna thought. A joke—that was all it was.

Gwen added, 'And of course fairytales just aren't very practical in the real world.'

Gianna put her fork down and reached an impulsive hand across to Gwen. 'I knew you'd understand,' she said. 'Blake and I—well, he's a wonderful person, but he's not exactly Prince Charming, and I'm no Sleeping Beauty——'

'Of course I know what you mean,' said Gwen. 'I'm so glad you're looking at it realistically, Gianna. Would you like some fresh fruit for dessert?'

Gianna glanced at her watch. 'I'm afraid I'll have to run,' she said. 'I've got some terribly important projects going on this afternoon.'

'At least you can take an apple with you,' Gwen said firmly.

When she returned with a basket of fruit, Gianna picked out a juicy Granny Smith and said, 'You know my weakness, don't you?'

'You were the first child I ever knew who'd turn down a cookie for an apple every time!'

At the door, Gianna kissed Gwen's soft, smooth cheek, and said, 'While we're talking of the Sleeping

Beauty—how long have you and Mom used Westway products?'

'Longer than I care to remember,' said Gwen with a grimace. 'John and Hal used us as guinea-pigs for the first batches of cold cream and cleansers. Why?'

'Because you both look so much younger than your age. I thought it would make a wonderful ad for the company—not only long and faithful users, but the very women who started it all.'

'Really, Gianna, spare my blushes!' laughed Gwen.

'I mean it, Gwen. I'm going to ask Blake about it this afternoon.' Gianna was delighted by the idea. 'I'm so glad we had this little talk!'

For more reasons than one, she thought as she drove back to the plant, munching on the apple. She'd been worrying more than she had realised about that crazy statement of Blake's. Now she could relax.

Trust Blake, she thought, to get it all wrong!

CHAPTER THREE

GIANNA glanced at the clock and swore. She had fifteen minutes to finish dressing; it would take another fifteen to reach the restaurant where they were to meet Cluny and Norman, and the damned zipper had got stuck in the back of her dress. Her best beige wool—the most flattering dress she had ever owned! She twisted around, trying to see over her shoulder into the mirror, and tugged gently. Nothing happened. She tugged harder, and was rewarded with the ominous sound of a stitch breaking.

She sighed and tried to pull the dress off over her head. It was a lost cause; she'd have to find something else to wear. It slid easily enough up over her shoulders, and then wouldn't budge another inch.

'Damn,' she said crossly. She worked it back down partway, so the collar wasn't smothering her any more, and tried to turn it so she could get a hand on the zipper. But the dress was binding around her arms, and now she couldn't even reach the little tag.

'Anybody home?' The cheerful call from the living-room brought relief.

'I need help, Blake!' she called.

She heard his footsteps coming across the hall. He stopped dead in her bedroom doorway, and said, 'I don't believe it. You were the one who was so excited about this date, and you're not even dressed!'

'I'm trying,' she said irritably. 'But I'm stuck. Would you help me out?'

'Let me think about it a minute,' said Blake. 'If I help you, I'll have to go with you tonight. If I don't, then I can plead ignorance. You certainly can't call Cluny to cancel, in that position.'

'Dammit, Blake——'

He laughed, and warm fingers turned her around so he could inspect the zipper. 'Hold still,' he said. 'What happened to your sense of humour?'

'It got cut off about the same time as my circulation did.'

He whistled tunelessly. 'You really have yourself stuck this time, kid!'

She stood patiently while he untangled the ravelled threads that had clogged the zipper's teeth. 'There,' he said as the catch slid free.

'Thanks, Blake.'

'Any time. I'm happy to be of service. Do you want it zipped up or down?'

'How badly is it ripped?' Gianna craned her neck to look at the damage.

'I can't see any gaps. Personally, I like it down. I think I'm behind the times, though,' he added. 'I thought girls still wore bras.'

Gianna whirled around to face him, her hands behind her back to hold the dress together. She had forgotten she hadn't bothered with a bra tonight. 'They do,' she said. 'I mean, mostly they do.'

'You're not wearing one.'

'It's not polite of you to look.'

'I could hardly avoid the sight. Would you like me to zip it back up?'

It would be indescribably silly of her to be missish, she decided. After all, she was wearing a slip under the scratchy wool. Why should she suddenly feel as if she was standing there without a stitch on?

And it would be senseless to insist on zipping the dress herself, and take the chance on getting it stuck again, when Blake could do the job easily. 'Please,' she said, and turned her back on him.

'I just had a brilliant idea,' said Blake. 'Marry me, and you'll never have to zip yourself up again.'

'Blake, don't be an idiot!' She ran a brush through her

hair and flipped the waves back over her shoulder.

He shrugged. 'And then you wouldn't have to worry about me seeing you without a bra, either.'

'It was only a back view. You don't need to start bragging about it!'

'What do you think I intend to do—post the news on the employee bulletin board?'

'I wouldn't put it past you,' said Gianna drily.

'I might as well. Most of our employees think we live together anyway.'

'Now that's sheer nonsense.' She flipped the switch that controlled the bathroom light, and the bulb popped, flared, and went dark, 'Damn!' she sighed.

'Why don't we just call this an ill-fated expedition and cancel?'

'Because you'll really like Cluny, once you get to know her.'

'Certain of that, aren't you?' said Blake curiously.

'Very. I've been meaning to talk to you, by the way. After dinner, why don't you take Cluny home? Norman will bring me back here, I'm sure——'

'You don't want anyone to invade your privacy, right? Why did you have to drag me in on this date at all?'

'I don't want to be alone with him. Or at any rate, I don't know him well enough to care whether we're alone. But I thought you and Cluny didn't need a chaperon.'

'Just what does Cluny do that a chaperon would frown on?' He sounded fascinated.

'Blake, really!'

'Well, if you insist on teaching me the facts of life, Gianna, you'll have to start with primary instruction.'

'You can't expect me to go into detail about Cluny's strong points; how in heaven's name would I know? But I understand she's a wonderful kisser. Do you have a spare light bulb, by the way?'

Blake patted his pockets, as if he half expected to find one, and then shook his head. 'Not on me, I'm afraid.'

Gianna made a small, irritated noise, and took her

make-up kit into the kitchen. 'This is ridiculous,' she muttered, and wet her eye-shadow brush under the tap. 'Trying to apply make-up in this light is impossible.' She looked up at Blake. 'You look great tonight, by the way.'

He straightened the handkerchief in the breast pocket of his muted tartan jacket, and bowed. 'Thank you.'

'You're a fraud,' she accused. 'Despite everything you've said, you really want to make a good impression on Cluny, don't you?'

'And how did you come to that conclusion?'

'You must,' she said. 'Or you wouldn't be wearing your new suit.'

Blake opened the refrigerator door. 'Do you have some antacid in here?'

'No. And you don't need any, anyway. You're only faking a stomach-ache—I know you. Have a glass of milk.'

Blake took a carton out, smelled it suspiciously, and said, 'Are you saving this till it turns into cottage cheese, or shall I throw it away now?'

'Why? Has it gone sour already?'

'I can't see why it should have,' he said mildly, tipping the contents down the drain. 'According to the date stamped on the carton, you've only owned it for nearly three weeks.'

'That's impossible.'

'Gianna, why would the milk carton lie? Why don't you marry me, then we wouldn't be wasting all this money on sour milk—we'd finish a carton before it spoiled. We would also only need to make one pot of coffee in the mornings, and——'

'I'm so glad you're enjoying your mother's joke,' she said coldly.

'Oh, I am. I might as well, because she isn't going to stop. It's no joke to her, Gianna.'

'It certainly is. I discussed it with her yesterday, and——'

'Yes, I know—I talked to her today. You thought she

agreed that the whole idea was silly. She thought you agreed that we were serious but weren't ready to talk about it just yet.'

Gianna stood by the kitchen sink, a lipstick brush dangling forgotten from her fingers. 'That's the stupidest thing I ever heard!'

'Quite possibly. Nevertheless, the two of you had a failure in communication.'

'How do you know?'

'After thirty years, I know what my mother is thinking. And she's thinking wedding bells.'

'But I'm sure I told her——'

Blake cleared his throat and looked at his watch. 'I certainly hate to be the one to bring it up, Gianna, but unless we leave now, we're going to be very late.'

Gianna rewarded him with a sunny smile. 'See? I knew that underneath it all you were looking forward to seeing Cluny.'

'No, dear. I just want to get the evening behind me.'

She ignored the interruption. 'You really ought to take Cluny out to meet your parents, Blake. That would let your mother see how ridiculous this notion of hers is. Not that I believe for an instant that she really thinks any such thing about the two of us——'

'Gianna.' It was soft, but there was a suggestion of iron underneath Blake's voice. 'Come on.'

Obediently she snapped the compact shut. 'For your information, Cluny would wait for ever for you.' She got her coat. 'I shouldn't tell you that, I suppose; it might make you conceited.'

'Then why tell me?'

'Because it's true. And besides, your biggest problem is a lack of self-confidence, Blake. I thought that knowing ahead of time that the lady thinks you're really special might help you relax.'

'Do you and Cluny spend a lot of time talking about me?' His tone was dry.

'Don't be silly. We've never actually spoken a word about it.'

'You haven't filled her in on all my little quirks? And it's only your opinion that she's wildly infatuated with me?'

'It's more than just an opinion, Blake. Women know when another woman is attracted to a man—they have a sixth sense about it. And believe me, I know how Cluny feels.'

'Because you're madly in love with me yourself, I suppose?'

Gianna giggled and gently pinched his cheek. 'You are cute when you're being shy,' she said.

'I'll try it. And remember, Gianna, you got me into this, and I'm going to have a great time if it kills you.'

'Don't fret! This evening will be more than you've ever dreamed of.'

Blake grunted. That, my dear,' he said, 'is exactly what terrifies me.'

Cluny and Norman were already at the restaurant, waiting in the outer lobby. Gianna caught sight of Cluny before the woman saw her. She's pacing the floor, she thought. Yes, they'll be a good pair. Blake was always on time, too, except when Gianna was holding him up.

She brushed her cheek against Cluny's. 'I'm so sorry we're late,' she said. 'It's entirely my fault.'

Cluny brushed the apology aside and turned the full beam of her charming smile on Blake.

'I hope you didn't mind waiting,' he said easily. 'Gianna got stuck in her dress, and I had to help her out of it.'

'You needn't make it sound quite that bad, Blake!' Gianna protested.

'Out of the situation, I meant,' Blake added. 'Not the dress.'

Cluny said smoothly, 'What a sweetheart you are, to be so helpful. I always knew you were something special,

Blake.' Her hand closed tightly on his arm, her dark red nails looking predatory against the muted shades of his jacket sleeve.

Blake sent a hunted look at Gianna, who smiled encouragingly at him before turning to look up at Norman, who had been watching her in worshipful silence. 'How are you tonight, Norman?' she asked.

Norman appeared to think it over, then he said bashfully, 'I'm fine, Gianna.' And he blushed.

Gianna sighed inwardly. Well, she thought, it was a small enough price to pay; an evening's boredom was worth it if it introduced Blake to an eligible woman. And Cluny was definitely that; she was really very nice, and she knew her way around society. She'd be quite an appropriate wife for Blake . . .

The evening turned out to be one of the shortest dates in the city's history. It was also, Gianna thought, the longest two hours that she had ever spent anywhere. The food at the new restaurant Cluny had chosen was mediocre; the lobster was tough and fishy-smelling, the steaks were uniformly grey, and the baked potatoes were rock-hard. Norman's company got no better as the evening progressed; carrying on a conversation with him was a challenge. Cluny fought hard to keep Blake's attention centred on herself, and made catty comments whenever he paid any attention to Gianna.

She's jealous of me, Gianna realised in astonishment, and wished there was some way to correct the woman's impressions before she made a complete fool of herself. She tried to pull Cluny away so she could tell her that, but Cluny refused to be separated from Blake.

Time after time the conversation—under Blake's guidance—found its way to business, with some important concern about Westway that couldn't wait till Monday to be discussed. Gianna tried her best to steer the talk back to general topics, but several times it was difficult to tear herself away from the more intriguing subjects Blake offered and go back to the inanities of talking to Norman. When she glared at Blake, trying to warn him off, he merely smiled and continued to discuss the problems of testing a new cleansing cream to prove that it would meet Federal regulations. The more he talked to Gianna, the cooler Cluny became.

It was a relief when the waiter poured their final cup of muddy coffee and brought the bill. By that time, Gianna was furious, Cluny was yawning, and Norman was still adoring. Blake alone was perfectly at ease.

Gianna picked up her bag and said, hating herself for the falsely cheerful note in her voice, 'You will see me home, won't you, Norman? I'm sure Blake and Cluny——'

Blake interrupted, 'I've been wanting all evening to tell you, Cluny, just how much I admire.' He took the woman's arm, and they strolled across the restaurant towards the main door.

Norman held Gianna's chair and whispered into her ear, 'I'm so glad you want me to take you home, Gianna.'

Gianna tried to hide her sigh, and hurried their steps to catch up with Blake and Cluny. They reached the lobby just in time to hear Blake say, 'I mean it, you know.' He was holding Cluny's fur coat, while they waited for the valet to return with his car.

Cluny blinked, as if unsure whether she was really hearing what he had said. Then she preened herself, and smiled.

Disgusting, Gianna thought.

Blake went on, 'I've been studying the way you've used your make-up to smooth the rough spots in your complexion, and to make your nose look narrower. You've done a very professional job, Cluny.'

Gianna put her hand to her forehead, where a sudden violent pain throbbed. Cluny's mouth was open in shock.

But Blake wasn't finished. 'And you've done a wonderful job in blending colours to cover the bags under your eyes,' he went on smoothly. 'You don't have bad ones, I can see, but you might want to try the new cover cream that we're bringing out. I think if you start using that, no one would even suspect that you have those dark circles.' He smiled down at her contentedly.

Cluny regained her voice. 'Norman, take me home. Now.'

'But, Cluny, I'm taking Gianna——'

'Norman!' There was no arguing with the icy voice. 'Get a cab—right now.'

'But, Cluny——' He gave up, and stepped out to the kerb, making a half-hearted gesture to a cruising cab.

'Allow me,' said Blake. He raised a hand, and the cab screeched to a halt.

Cluny glared at Gianna. 'Thanks for nothing!' she hissed.

'I'm sorry if you're not feeling well, Cluny,' Blake said solicitously, as he helped her into the cab. 'You've looked a bit pale, but I thought perhaps a different shade of foundation was all it would take. I hope another time we can do the nightclubs?'

'I doubt it.' Cluny said tightly. She was looking straight ahead. 'In fact, don't bother to call me—I won't be at home.'

'Oh. Well, I'm very sorry you feel that way.' His voice trailed off. 'I only meant it as a compliment, you know——' He waved the cab off, watched it out of sight down the street, and returned to Gianna's side. 'I don't know what happened,' he explained. 'I guess you're stuck with me after all.'

'You don't know what happened?' said Gianna. Each word was separate, distinct, emphatic. 'You did that deliberately, Blake Whittaker!'

He looked astounded. 'I haven't any idea what you mean. I only complimented her on her use of make-up——'

'In the many years I've known you, Blake, I've never heard you say anything quite that crass, said Gianna acidly. 'You just don't tell somebody that she did a fairly good job of covering up the dark bags under her eyes, dammit!'

'Well, I think it now and then,' said Blake. The doorman pulled the car up, and he helped Gianna in.

'That is entirely beside the point!'

'Do you think she'll ever forgive me?'

His tone was meek, but she didn't believe a word of it. 'Never. And that's just the way you planned it, too, isn't it? Admit it, Blake!'

He looked slightly ashamed of himself, but she knew he was faking that, too. She turned her back on him, as well as she could in the limited space of the small car. It was really a shame, she thought. Blake was such a nice guy, such a wonderful friend, that she couldn't bear the thought that he might always be alone like this.

She trampled that sympathetic thought. See if I ever help arrange a date for him again! she thought. If he was foolish enough not to appreciate the efforts of his best friend——

'You're a graceless scamp,' she said.

He looked properly chastened, and was silent the rest of the way home. As the elevator reached their floor, he said mournfully, 'And I didn't even get the goodnight kiss you promised.'

'Well, don't for heaven's sake look at *me*,' Gianna said crossly. 'I don't plan to supply the deficiency. It was your own fault, anyway. Cluny would have been happy to oblige, until your little lecture about the proper use of cover-up creams.'

'You don't have to be unsympathetic,' Blake protested.

Gianna didn't dignify that with a comment.

'There must be something wrong with my technique,' he speculated.

That has nothing to do with it. Cluny didn't even get close enough to find out what your technique is.'

'Perhaps all I need is practice,' Blake said hopefully. He looked down at her, and his hazel eyes sparkled. 'You wouldn't refuse to help out an old friend, would you?'

'And kiss you?' Gianna's voice was squeaky with shock. She tried to steady it, and looked up at him. His handsome face was bent close to hers, the dark arch of eyebrows slightly lifted. What would it be like to kiss him? she wondered breathlessly.

Like kissing your big brother, she reminded herself. There was no excitement to that.

She fumbled in her handbag for her key, and turned away from him to insert it in the lock. 'Don't be ridiculous, Blake,' she said. 'Practising with me wouldn't do you any good. There's no sense in kissing someone you're not attracted to.'

He sighed. 'I didn't think you'd be the kind to turn your back on a friend, Gianna.' But he didn't push the subject, and she was glad. There, for a minute, it had seemed to her as if the man who had been her friend all these years had silently slipped away, and left a stranger in his place.

She looked up at him with puzzlement in her eyes. 'Don't you ever get lonely, Blake?' she asked.

He put a finger under her chin and smiled down into her eyes. 'Yes, dear. But stop trying to fix me up. Women like Cluny are just not in my book at all.'

She had to admit that Cluny hadn't helped matters. If she hadn't been so catty, and had hidden her boredom, Blake might not have done what he had. But still—— 'By the time you get around to settling down, all the women your age will be dead!' she said tartly.

He laughed. 'Don't worry, Gianna. In the meantime, there's always television and other hobbies to keep me occupied. Want to watch an old Humphrey Bogart film tonight?' He consulted his wristwatch. 'It starts in half an hour.'

'Blake, you're incorrigible!'

'I'll even make the popcorn,' he added.

'Is that why you wanted to hurry home? To watch an old movie?'

'Besides,' Blake reminded her, 'you can't get out of that

dress without help.'

That brought a smile. 'Caramel corn,' she bargained.

'Nope. Ordinary—it's better for your figure.'

'And what's wrong with my figure?' she challenged.

He flicked her cheek with a careless finger. 'Nothing, yet. That's why you're staying with ordinary popcorn.'

'You just don't want to bother with making the caramel sauce.'

He smiled and didn't argue the point. 'Make a decision, Gianna. Am I coming in or not?'

She sighed. 'In,' she said. She closed the door behind him. What was there about Blake, she wondered, that made it so hard to argue with him? He seldom made a fuss, and yet he almost always got his way.

It would be the same, she thought, whenever he did find the woman of his dreams. She wouldn't stand a chance—in the opposite sort of way from the fiasco tonight. Cluny Brown couldn't have held his attention tonight if she'd jumped out of a cake naked.

For a moment, Gianna felt something almost like sympathy for the woman Blake would eventually choose. Stubborn—that was the only word for him. Stubborn—and unpredictable as well.

The interview had been arranged long since; the reporter from the metropolitan newspaper had called weeks before. Her talk with Gianna, she said, would end up as part of a series on women around Chicago who were making a success of their own businesses.

Gianna wasn't certain that she really fitted the category; since her share of Westway had been passed down to her by her father, she had only built on his achievements, not created something of her own. But the reporter had assured her that women like Gianna were precisely what the newspaper's readers wanted to hear about, and so she had, uneasily, agreed to be interviewed.

Now that it was too late to back out, she sat at her desk, cradling a cup of coffee in her hands, and watched the reporter, who took an occasional sip from her own mug in between jotting notes.

Unusual, she thought, to send, on an interview like this, a reporter who apparently never used cosmetics at all. The woman's clothes were rumpled and cheap-looking, and her hair was mussed. Gianna thought, And she's reporting on glamour? She could use a little herself!

The first questions were simple—background facts about Gianna, and details about the company. It absorbed quite a lot of time, and Gianna was beginning to think the story would end up to be no more than a *Who's Who* entry. Then the reporter looked up over the rim of her cup and said, 'One of the founders of Westway was once quoted as saying that a company based on a woman's vanity couldn't possibly fail.'

'Hal Whittaker said that,' Gianna told her. 'I don't believe he intended it for publication.'

'Nevertheless, he seemed to think it illustrated the company's philosophy. Is that still true today?'

This was tricky ground. Gianna sipped her coffee and said slowly, 'Hal made that comment about thirty years ago. The company was very new then, and its main products were lipstick, rouge, and perfumes.'

The reporter looked up, her pale eyes unfriendly behind round lenses. 'That doesn't answer the question, Miss West.'

'If you'll give me a moment, I'll be happy to finish my answer. Today, things are much different, not only with the company, but with the world. Most women today don't have time to be vain—and it isn't vanity, anyway, for a woman to want to look her best. It's a necessity, if she has a job of any sort. And I include in that the very real career of raising children and being a full-time homemaker.'

'I don't quite follow your point,' the reporter said earnestly. 'Are you saying that a woman has to use make-up to be successful?'

'No. But I believe that a woman who looks her best,

and knows it, will feel her best, and that will reflect in her job.'

The reporter scribbled. 'You mentioned changes in the company?'

'Yes. Long ago Westway began a line of skin-care products that emphasised long-term health, and not just good looks for today. Many of the cosmetics used at that time were skin-drying, and after years of use some of them actualy damaged the complexion. Over the past few years, we've introduced easy-to-use versions of our skin care products that even the busiest of women can find time to apply.'

'So the company philosophy now is——?'

Gianna hesitated, then said thoughtfully, 'We want our hypothetical woman to look her best this morning when she leaves for work, tonight when she goes out to dinner, and in thirty years, when her skin will still be soft and supple and—we hope—without a wrinkle. And we want her to be able to care for her skin in ten minutes a day.'

'That sounds like a guarantee. You use it yourself, of course?'

Gianna laughed, and brushed her knuckles along the soft line of her jaw. 'Can't you tell?'

The reporter didn't share the joke. 'And you believe that make-up can make a woman successful?'

'Not make-up—skin care,' Gianna reminded her. 'We produce a line for men, too, by the way.' She paused, then plunged in. She might some day regret saying this, she thought, but it was worth the effort to make this cynical reporter understand. 'I believe that in the business world when a man begins to show his age, we say he's distinguished. When a woman begins to show her age, we say she's getting old. In an ideal world, things wouldn't be like that—but they are. You know it, and I know it, and every woman who's ever held a job knows it. We're just doing a little bit to even the odds, that's all.'

Blake opened the door. 'Sorry to bother you,' he said

when he saw the woman sitting across from Gianna. He looked a little curious. 'But I'm leaving now, and I didn't want you to forget our date tonight, Gianna.'

Giana could have cried, or thrown something at him. She had spent the last hour establishing herself as a responsible businesswoman with the authority to speak for women in general, and in fifteen seconds, Blake had blasted her out of the water!

It had been a meaningful choice of words, a way to give her the message without coming out in the open with it. He could have said, 'Don't forget that we're meeting Meghan and her manager for a drink tonight,' which would have given the reporter a scoop beyond anything she had ever dreamed of.

You should be happy he didn't give anything away, she told herself. It didn't help; she still wanted to take off her high-heeled shoe and throw it at him. A date, indeed! She had a nosy reporter sitting in her office, and Blake announced that they had a date!

The reporter looked intrigued. Gianna sighed and introduced them, and Blake shook hands cheerfully and left, very fast, as if he didn't want to stay and watch the fireworks.

Lucky Blake, Gianna thought. At least he didn't have to answer questions!

She said, before the reporter had a chance to go on, 'There is one other point I'd like to make in answer to your original question, about the company being based on vanity. We now earn almost half our gross revenue from other kinds of products—not our beauty and skin-care lines at all. We make toothpaste, for example, at our plant in Tennessee. We also produce mouthwash, shampoo, and suntan lotion. They're not as glamorous, and so not as much is said about them. But they're just as necessary.'

The reporter nodded, and obediently made a few notes. 'A noted stock-market analyst recommended Westway as a good growth investment a few weeks ago,' she said. 'In fact, the headline in his newsletter read, "Go Westway, Young Man". Do you have any comment on that?'

Gianna smiled, a little relieved that the situation had been defused. 'Yes. That's a dreadful pun. I think he's very perceptive about the company, though.'

'Any new products to be announced soon?'

'There are always things in research and development. Nothing that I'm able to talk about at the moment, though.' It was winding down, she thought; the last few questions were always easy.

'You spoke very movingly a few minutes ago about women who are full-time homemakers. Do you have any plans to become one of them?'

Gianna West as a full-time homemaker? For a moment, she wished Blake hadn't been in such a hurry to leave. He would have seen the humour in that question.

'Certainly not any time soon,' she answered, 'and probably not ever. Westway is a very important part of my life, and I don't think I could give it up entirely. Besides, I see no reason to do so. Any man I might be interested in marrying would understand how important the company is to me.'

'What about your relationship with your partner?'

'With Blake?' Gianna asked uneasily. The question sounded innocent; if it hadn't been for Blake's comment about them having a date, and the twist the reporter had given some of her answers, she wouldn't have given it a thought. 'Blake and I have a wonderful working partnership. And we're very good friends,' she added.

'Very good friends,' the reporter repeated thoughtfully.

'That's right. We grew up together, you know.'

'I see. Which of you earns more?'

'Is that really pertinent to the story?'

The reporter shrugged. 'Probably only if he earns more.'

Gianna gave in. 'We draw equal salaries. His official

title is Chairman of the board, mine is President. We split the duties of the chief executive officer right down the middle.'

'And that works?' The reporter wrinkled her nose doubtfully.

'I wouldn't recommend it as a management style for most people, no. But Blake and I are ideally suited. Our strengths fit together like the pieces of a puzzle, you see. I have the ideas, and he keeps me from going overboard.'

The reporter glanced at the closed door, then at Gianna, and smiled. 'I see,' she said softly. 'Thank you for your time, Miss West. May I call if I have further questions?'

Giana saw her out, then sagged into her chair. She felt like a limp dishrag from the effort she had put in. And she still had an evening with Meghan ahead.

She sighed, and pushed her chair back. There was no point in trying to work any more this afternoon; it would take every moment she had left to make herself presentable. At that, she could never compete with Meghan's effortless beauty—but at least she could put up a better front than she must present at the moment.

Besides, she thought, with Blake already gone, no one would complain if she sneaked out of the office early.

She wondered what he'd had to do this afternoon that was so very important, and grinned. Perhaps he too was trying to look his best, to impress Meghan!

'I can't blame him,' she said to herself. 'Poor Cluny. No wonder she didn't stand a chance!'

CHAPTER FOUR

MEGHAN and her manager were late.

Gianna sipped her second glass of wine, and glanced at her watch. 'Wouldn't you think the woman would at least be on time?' she asked irritably. 'I mean, she is supposed to be professional——'

Blake raised an eyebrow. 'Coming from you, Gianna, that's a joke!'

'I'm usually on time,' she said irritably. 'It's only the rare occasion——'

'Fortunately for you, company policy says that executives don't have to punch a time clock,' Blake went on ruthlessly. 'If you did, you'd be out a couple of hours' pay every week.'

'We were not discussing me,' Gianna pointed out.

He grinned. 'Why shouldn't we? Are you getting uncomfortable? Anyway, why should Meghan worry about being on time? Who's going to complain about waiting for Meghan?'

'I should think some of those high-priced photographers would.'

Blake shook his head. 'Not if they're men.'

She looked up at him curiously. 'You really do have a thing about Meghan, don't you? Maybe you ought to give it a try, Blake. I've never heard anything about a man in her life. You could be famous as the man who captured the elusive Meghan——'

'And what would Meghan see in me that would make her inclined to be captured?'

'You're joking!' Gianna set her wine glass down with a little thump. 'You're a sweet guy, you're very good-looking, you're moderately rich—and you wonder what a woman could see in you?'

'Of course not. I was just fishing for compliments, Gianna.'

'That's what I thought.'

'But at least she's a better choice than Cluny was.'

'I saw Cluny yesterday, by the way. She was coming out of a boutique at Water Tower Place.' Gianna stared into her wine glass.

'And?'

'And she scarcely spoke to me. She did send you a message, however.'

'Oh?'

'Yes. She said to tell you that it didn't matter how many flowers you sent, you were still a conceited, boring, arrogant—well, I can't remember the rest. You get the drift of it.'

Blake sighed. 'So much for my attempts to pacify Cluny!'

'What did you send her, anyway?' asked Gianna. 'Dandelions?'

'Roses. A dozen of them.'

'You astonish me. I thought for a minute she was going to push me down the escalator, just for being a witness to that disaster.'

'It would have served you right.'

'What did I do that was so awful?' asked Gianna. 'All I did was try to bring together two people I thought might enjoy knowing each other——'

'Stick to cosmetics,' Blake recommended. 'You're much better at that than you are as a matchmaker.'

'But I'm concerned about you, Blake.'

'Of course, you could always do something nice for my mother——'

'And marry you myself? No, thanks, dear. I'm not into sacrifices, not even to please your mother.'

'It would have advantages for you,' he pointed out.

'Like what?'

'You could stop spending all your time trying to fix me up with a date, then. Plus we could cut our rent and utility bills in half. And we could get our health insurance cheaper.'

'The company already pays it.'

Blake ignored the interruption. 'We wouldn't have to give the doorman two gifts at Christmas time any more. We could even get family rates on our season tickets.'

Gianna sipped her wine and said sweetly. 'Blake, what would you do if I said yes?'

'Die of shock, right here on the spot,' he said promptly.

'Then don't worry. I wouldn't want to cause you any pain.'

'But think about what a great benefit it would be for all our friends,' he said. 'They could send us one invitation instead of two to all the parties.'

'To say nothing of the benefit to your budget, since you wouldn't have to buy roses for people like Cluny any more.'

'That's true. I hadn't thought of that. Don't you realise that we're the perfect combination, Gianna? You wouldn't even have to change the monogram on your luggage.'

Gianna had stoppedBZlistening. She was looking across the room. 'My God, she's beautiful!' she exclaimed.

Meghan's entrance had not been announced, but suddenly every eye in the place was riveted on her. The model glided across the room, looking somehow as if she wasn't moving at all, her long body draped in a deceptively simple white sheath, her black hair in a classic knot at the back of her neck. She wore no jewellery. There was nothing about her to draw attention away from that striking face, the sultry eyes, the sensual lips.

'Not bad,' said Blake. The words were casual, but there was a husky catch in his voice that startled Gianna.

She glanced up at him, a little shocked. He was watching Meghan.

My goodness, she thought, he does have it bad, after all! She turned to stare again at Meghan. The woman must be one of the half-dozen in the world who truly looked good in pure, plain white, she thought resentfully. It wasn't fair for Meghan to have it all—brains, beauty, fame and fortune——

The man with Meghan pulled out a chair for her. Gianna hadn't even noticed him until then; he had been no more noticeable than a piece of the wallpaper.

Blake, you missed your chance to impress her with what a gentleman you are, she thought a little spitefully. You could have been the one who seated her.

Blake had risen, though, and reached across the table to shake the manager's hand. 'Glad you could join us, Curtis,' he said. 'Gianna, Curtis Jones.'

The manager nodded, and introduced them. Blake said something about what a pleasure it was to meet the marvellous Meghan. Gianna decided he'd probably practised the line into his mirror all afternoon, to get the alliteration just right.

Meghan didn't even answer. She merely lowered her eyelids, very slowly, till the long black lashes swept against her high cheekbones. The gesture was like a courtly bow. Then she raised her lids again, and the sudden reappearance of her luminescent deep green eyes made Gianna gasp. She could imagine the effect that it had on Blake . . .

Almost any man, she thought, would have reeled at the naked intimacy in that glance. But especially Blake——

It made Gianna a little uneasy. Blake wasn't exactly inexperienced, she told herself firmly. There had always been women, and yet he had never dated any one of them steadily. A woman who was on the prowl would have little difficulty in taming Blake. And a woman like Meghan, who could have any man in the world at her feet—— Well, if a woman like Meghan chose to go after Blake, he wouldn't stand a chance.

Gianna glanced at him, wanting to catch his eye. Perhaps she was only being silly, and they would look at each other and burst into laughter at the very idea that he might be a mere minnow in Meghan's net.

But try as she might, Gianna could not get his attention. Blake was ignoring her. He was absorbed in Meghan, watching as she sipped her Perrier water and batted her eyelashes at him over the rim of her glass.

No, Gianna told herself, that wasn't quite accurate. Meghan didn't bat her eyelids; she did nothing quite that crude. It was a mere flutter, playing with those incredible green eyes. And it was very effective, Gianna was forced to admit.

'You don't live here in Chicago, do you, Meghan?' she asked.

Very slowly, Meghan transferred her attention to Gianna. She sipped her water and appeared to think the question over before saying, 'No.'

'Do you spend much time here? In your work, I mean.'

The answer was a little faster this time. 'Not much.'

'Where are you from, originally?'

A longer pause. 'The South.'

That explained the slow speech, the hint of an accent that had, at first, sounded slightly foreign. But the fact that she had finally got an answer of sorts didn't make Gianna any more comfortable. I feel like an idiot, she thought. I asked three simple questions, and got nowhere. Doesn't the woman know how to carry on a conversation, or is she just discouraging any competition from the other female at the table?

Meghan's manager laughed. 'That's my mystery girl,' he said fondly. 'Don't take it personally, Miss West. Meghan feels very strongly about her privacy.'

'I can see that,' Gianna said sourly.

Blake had leaned across the table towards Meghan. 'Do you enjoy your work?' he asked softly.

She glowed like a fire that had just had a bellows applied. 'Oh, yes,' she said ingenuously. 'I really like the travel, and I think it's marvellous to be able to work with all these wonderful men. They're so talented with their cameras. Why, they can even make me look beautiful!'

Gianna thought she was going to be sick.

The manager beamed. 'Meghan's modesty is one of the things I just can't believe about her,' he confided.

.'Likewise,' Gianna said tartly. She noticed that Blake's hand was lying on the pristine tablecloth right next to Meghan's, and that the model hadn't moved a millimetre. They'll be holding hands in a minute, she thought irritably. Well, it's obvious that Blake isn't interested in the difficult questions. I guess if they're going to be asked, I'll have to ask them.

'We will need a little information before we go any further with negotiations,' she pointed out.

The manager nodded. 'That's what I'm here for,' he said, 'Meghan never bothers her head with business details.'

'Well, she's fortunate to have you, Curtis. If there's anything embarrassing in Meghan's past, we need to know about it now.'

Curtis frowned. 'Like what?'

'Oh, for instance—any photos of her in the nude.'

He looked horrified. 'Oh, Meghan would never have done anything like that!'

'You'd be surprised at the girls who would, and who have,' Giana told him drily. 'There's a point, when a model is trying to become established, when she'll do nearly anything. She might even act in a less than tasteful movie, for the money and for the boost it's supposed to be to her acting career.'

'Oh, some day Meghan will be an actress,' Curtis assured her. 'Won't that face be dynamite on the big screen? We're in no hurry, though. She's working with a drama coach, and in another year or two, when she's ready, there'll be a Hollywood epic written just for her.'

'The kind of film I'm thinking of wouldn't exactly have been called an epic,' Gianna said. 'Though it could do epic damage to her career. If we come to an agreement on this deal, Curtis, Meghan will be asked to sign a contract, and part of that will be an assurance that she's done nothing of the sort that might embarrass Westway.'

'Meghan would never——'

Gianna cut him off. 'If I were you I'd do some investigating of my own, Curtis. Just to be certain that there aren't any skeletons that might fall out of closets at the wrong time.'

He looked a bit put out. 'If you aren't going to take my word for it——'

'Of course we will,' Gianna said gently. 'On a contract. But I'd like to be sure you really know what you're agreeing to. You might also check into any possible legal problems——'

'You can't be implying that Meghan might be involved in anything illegal!'

'I'm not accusing her of smuggling diamonds, Curtis. I just don't want to find out later that she's been arrested for driving while intoxicated in South Podunk Center— or Chicago, for that matter.'

He drew himself up. 'Meghan doesn't drink.'

'I'm charmed!'

'Consuming alcohol isn't good for her complexion. Surely *you* ought to know that?'

'You'd be amazed, Curtis, at the number of women who know it, but go right ahead and apply it internally, anyway. At any rate, do us both a favour and check it out. We don't want any embarrassing incidents coming out in the middle of an expensive ad campaign.'

'No one else has ever made these sorts of personal demands on Meghan before,' sniffed Curtis.

Gianna refused to be disturbed. 'You must remember that we aren't just using Meghan in our ads, we're identifying our product with her name. In most of her work, if something discredited Meghan, the company would simply find another model. In some cases, the added publicity would even be welcome. But for us, it would mean sacrificing the product. Of course we're going to be a little more careful, and avoid anything embarrassing.'

'Embarrassing?' Meghan said softly, from across the table. She was wide-eyed. 'Curtis, perhaps you'd better tell her about that afternoon I——' She stopped, and her slender hand went to her throat. A very becoming blush crept over her angular face.

'Oh, that was nothing, Meghan,' Curtis dismissed with a wave of his hand. 'That's not the sort of thing we're talking about at all.'

Well, thought Gianna. For once, Meghan and I are on the same side of the fence! 'I think you'd better tell me, Curtis,' she said.

'It's nothing of the kind you're talking about,' he said. 'Meghan was a little embarrassed afterwards, I grant you, but it was certainly nothing illegal.'

Gianna shifted in her chair. 'Curtis, I don't think you quite understand——'

Blake's hand clamped on her arm. 'That's enough, Gianna. I'll take care of this.'

She was furious. 'Why, you——' She caught herself, and decided not to get involved in a public brawl with her partner. She would just wait till morning and take him apart in the privacy of her office.

She sat silent for a moment, trying unsuccessfully to swallow her anger. It didn't work. She needed a few minutes by herself, she decided. 'If you would excuse me for a moment?' she said icily, and rose, hoping against hope that Meghan wouldn't feel it necessary to accompany her to the ladies' room. If she does, she told herself, I'll lock myself in the litle cubicle and refuse to come out!

But Meghan stayed firmly in her chair. She doesn't want to leave the men, Gianna decided. There were women like that, who couldn't abide the company of another female. That must be why Meghan hadn't answered her questions, but had bubbled to Blake like a little fountain . . .

Gianna reached the safety of the ladies' room with a sigh of relief, and sank into a velvet chair. Damn, she thought. It was bad enough when Blake had abdicated all responsibility; it had, after all, been his idea to ask about the embarrassing moments of Meghan's life. But then, when Gianna had taken over the job, for him to tell her to mind her own business——

Well, there's one thing about it, she thought. This might have been my idea, but I haven't signed any contracts yet. And if I don't get satisfactory answers to my questions, that's the end of that. We'll look for someone else to promote our product, and little Miss Meghan and her marvellous manager can go straight back to wherever she came from and stay there.

'I wonder what it was she did on that mysterious afternoon,' she mused. She let her imagination roam. Meghan might have been caught shoplifting. Or perhaps she had assaulted someone. Or perhaps——

The door of the ladies' room opened, and a burst of music from the dance floor poured in. A snide voice asked, 'Are you sulking in here, Gianna?'

She looked up, startled. 'Oh. Hi, Cluny,' she said warily. 'No, I'm not sulking. What gave you that idea?'

'I suspected you might be. The press caught up with your guest out there, and I thought it possible that you were upset to have been missed.'

'The press? I suppose we should have expected that.' Blake, you idiot! she thought. Why couldn't you have chosen some private place to meet Meghan and Curtis? Or, she wondered, had Blake selected this busy spot on purpose, so that he would be seen with the glamorous model? Not Blake, she decided. He had too much common sense for that.

Cluny was watching her with satisfaction in the mirror, as she drew a cupid's bow on her lips.

'I suppose we'd better get out of here,' Gianna murmured, to herself.

'You don't need to be in any hurry,' purred Cluny.

'What do you mean?'

'Just that the lady has gone. It must be awful, having to

live that way—always pursued.'

'Well, I hope Blake doesn't blame me,' muttered Gianna, and bit her tongue. She ought to have more sense than to say anything of the kind in front of Cluny!

'He didn't seem to mind,' Cluny shrugged. 'He looked quite happy to be escorting her.'

'Blake? Blake took her home?'

Cluny raised an arched eyebrow. 'Oh, he didn't desert you altogether, if that's what you're concerned about. The other gentlemen is waiting at your table.'

Gianna could have cried. In this frame of mind, Blake might do anything——

She seized her key and hurried out, painfully aware of the satisfied smile that Cluny wore.

The woman had been right. Only Curtis waited at their table. Meghan's glass had been deserted half-full, and the waiter was just refilling Blake's wine glass in front of his empty chair.

'He's left,' Curtis told the waiter, just as Gianna reached the table.

'Where did they go?' she asked.

He shrugged. 'Search me. Some kind of a dance club. Blake said he knew some place quiet where Meghan wouldn't be bothered.'

'I'll bet he does,' Gianna said grimly. It could be any one of twenty places, and it would be a hopeless task to try to track him down. If he had wanted to disappear, he couldn't have done a better job. Now she wouldn't be able to talk to him till morning.

And perhaps, she thought, he had planned it that way—had seized the opportunity presented by the cameras and Gianna's absence to sweep Meghan away and have her to himself. An opportunity every man in the country dreamed of—an evening spent dancing with Meghan . . .

Meghan, Gianna told herself, is the single dullest woman I've ever encountered. She can't carry on a conversation—or won't. She bats those big green eyes and makes the man of the moment think he's being worshipped.

And the entire male half of the population fell promptly into the trap, too, she reminded herself. Blake included.

Perhaps dull is what a man really wants, she thought. He can convince himself that, if Meghan finds him suitable to worship, he must be really something.

Poor Blake, she thought.

'I'm sure we'll be meeting again,' she told Curtis.

'Aren't you going to have another drink?' He reached across the table for Blake's wine glass. 'It's a pity to waste this.'

What's the point? Gianna thought. The bird I was hunting has flown. She shook her head.

Curtis sighed. 'Then I'll take you home.'

'I wouldn't want you to waste that wine,' she said briefly. 'I can get a cab.'

Curtis had drunk the wine by the time the battle of wills was over. Gianna won, but only by being slightly rude. She didn't quite know why it was so important to her to escape, to be alone, but she knew that she did not want to invite Curtis up to her apartment for a cup of coffee and the standard wrestling match. She also knew that if she let him take her home, he would expect nothing less for his trouble. She had met Curtis's kind before. So she stood firm and got into the taxi alone.

Her apartment was quiet and cold. She turned the thermostat up, shivering in her thin wool dress. Had the heat gone out? For an instant, she actually considered calling Blake to find out if his apartment also was without heat, before she remembered that Blake— wherever he was—was certainly not feeling the cold. No man who was basking in the warmth of Meghan's smile could be bothered to notice the temperature.

She put a frozen dinner in the oven, and fleetingly thought about climbing in with it, where it was warm. Instead, she changed into jeans and three layers of sweaters, and went back to the kitchen to brew herself a cup of tea. Then she made her regular weekly call to her parents.

Her father answered the telephone, and greeted her enthusiastically. 'We've got our tickets,' he told her. 'We'll be flying into O'Hare two weeks from today, Gianna.'

'That's great! I'll be there to pick you up.'

'We'll be staying a week,' said Carol, on the extension phone. 'Gwen said you might come out to stay at the house?'

'For part of the week, at least.'

'Come for the whole time,' John West said expansively. 'It'll be handier for you to get to the office, anyway.'

Gianna laughed. 'It is Gwen's house, you know, Dad. She invited me for a few days.'

'She won't mind. I always did think Gwen was a mother hen who would have liked a dozen chicks.'

'Gianna,' her mother said, 'you sound a little odd. Are you coming down with a cold?'

'If I was it would be no wonder. The heat has gone off in my apartment.'

'Honey,' ordered Carol, 'you go ask Blake to check it out, right away!'

'I will, Mom.' There was no point in explaining the situation, that was for sure. It was pretty unrealistic of Carol to assume that Blake had nothing better to do than sit around and wait for Gianna to call him. She would wait a while, and if he didn't get home, she'd call the supervisor.

'We don't want you getting pneumonia,' John added.

'I'm grown up, now, Daddy, remember? What flight number will you be on?' She copied the numbers down on the back of her grocery list, and turned the conversation to Christmas. It was obvious, she thought as she put the telephone down, how much her parents were looking forward to an old-fashioned holiday with all the people they most cared about around them.

The last few years, Gianna had made the trip to Florida each December, and spent part of her holiday lying on the beach. But it wasn't like the old days, and sometimes a week or two off didn't fit very well into the work that needed doing at the company. Perhaps this was the best solution possible.

She hadn't even put up a tree the last few years; she hadn't been around enough to enjoy it. Perhaps this year she would go and buy a small tree, just enough to bring the holiday spirit into her apartment. Maybe Blake would come over some evening and help her decorate it—if he wasn't too busy with Meghan.

The instantaneous thought disturbed her. After all, it wasn't as if there was anything serious going on. Blake had only taken the girl out for an evening of dancing, and that was incidental to the business he was trying to transact. He probably wouldn't ever see her again socially, and he was determined to enjoy this evening. How many men would give their right arms to be in Blake Whittaker's shoes tonight!

She ate her dinner, picking at the beef Stroganoff. She'd had too much wine before dinner, she thought; it was no wonder she was seeing things from a skewed point of view.

The apartment was getting colder. She turned the thermostat up again, knowing that it would make no difference, anyway, and checked her watch. She might as well call the super, she thought. It was anybody's guess as to when Blake would be home.

She was dialling the number when there was a knock on her door. She put the telephone down and went to answer it, then released the chain and opened the door wide. 'Am I ever glad to see you!' she said thankfully.

Blake scratched his head. 'You've been thinking over my proposal, and you've decided to accept?' he asked, sounding a little hesitant.

'I wouldn't do that to my best friend.'

'Then why were you so eager to see me?'

'Because the heat's off and I'm freezing,' she explained. 'Have you been to your place yet?'

'No. Is the whole building out of commission?'

'I don't know.'

'Well, let's start here.' He tossed his jacket across a chair. 'You weren't kidding, were you? It's bitterly cold in this room.'

'I was just about to call the supervisor.'

'I always knew there was something wrong with my timing,' mused Blake. He tinkered with the thermostat. 'It helps if you turn the heat on, Gianna.'

'It is,' she told him.

'Nope. You must have clicked the little switch off some time.' He gave it a push. 'It doesn't matter if you have the thermostat set at ninety-three, if the instructions can't get to the main system.'

'Oh.' She looked at the switch, and then up at him. 'I don't remember ever doing that, Blake.'

'I didn't expect you would.'

Warm air was pouring out of the vents, and Gianna rubbed her hands gratefully in the stream. 'Thanks, Blake. You're home early, aren't you?'

'Meghan's shooting tomorrow,' he explained. 'She needs her sleep.'

'Of course—I should have known.'

She had done her best to cover up any sarcasm in her tone, but Blake looked at her oddly anyway. 'What did you think of Curtis, Gianna?' he asked.

'I think Curtis has an inflated opinion of his own importance. In fact, I think if Curtis hadn't been born at all, he'd be expecting people all over the world to ask why.'

Blake said, 'I see. I was sorry to leave you there alone, but it was getting to be a circus. The poor girl was being besieged for autographs——'

'She has all my sympathy!'

'I knew you'd understand. What did you think of her, Gianna?'

He sounded as eager as a boy. She remembered an occasion when they had been teenagers and Blake had introduced her to the new girl of his dreams. There had been that same eagerness in his voice, that same desire to have someone else share his enthusiasm. Giana had to admit that it was easier to understand this time; there was no competition between Meghan and that slightly overweight and pimply teenage girl . . .

'I've heard of guys taking a dive for a pretty face before, Blake,' she said, 'but you take the prize!'

He blinked. 'Do you think she is?'

'Is what?'

'Just a pretty face. Meghan strikes me as a lovely woman, and a professional. And yet she isn't conceited at all.'

Gianna looked at him in astonishment, Her mouth slightly open. 'Blake, I'm trying to tell you I think we should run for the nearest exit. This isn't going to work!'

'Why not?'

'I just don't think Meghan is quite——'

'Why not? What possible objections can you have?'

'Oh, for starters, I'd like to know just what it was she did on that embarrassing afternoon,' said Gianna.

'That's easy enough. She told me.' Blake settled himself in an easy chair. She ate three banana splits in an hour. It was a binge, you see——'

Gianna stared at him. Then, carefully, she said, 'That's what Meghan considers embarrassing?'

'Wouldn't you? She's a model, for heaven's sake. She can't afford to be fat, or to leave the impression that she's anything but happy with her body as it is——'

'Three banana splits? I thought it must have been attempted murder, at least!'

Blake looked disgusted. 'Gianna, you have a cynical twist to your mind. Meghan is an innocent child.'

'I wouldn't bet on it, if she's spent any time at all hanging around with Curtis,' said Gianna drily. 'No, I'm not going to get into an argument.'

'Well, she's the perfect choice for the new perfume.'

'Too bad. I won't go along with it.'

'You can't back out,' Blake said. 'We've already made a verbal agreement with Meghan.'

'Blake, there's been nothing signed——'

'What's the matter with you, Gianna?' He looked astounded. 'It's going to be a wonderful promotion. And after all, my dear—it was your idea.'

And that, Gianna thought, was the worst thing of it all. If it worked, he'd take the credit for carrying through with the plan. If it didn't, she'd get the blame because it had been her idea.

And in the meantime, she was stuck with Meghan.

CHAPTER FIVE

GIANNA tried, in the two weeks that followed, to convince Blake that she really did know what she was talking about, that her instinct said they would get in trouble if they pursued this scheme.

Each time she said it, Blake merely looked at her as if she'd gone completely crazy, repeated that they were now committed, and reminded her that it had orignally been her idea, and that he thought it was a good one.

That was part of the problem, she wanted to tell him. Blake never made mistakes in matters like this. Surely he wouldn't have fallen in with this idea if it had been totally hare-brained? And yet she just couldn't quite bring herself to trust him on this one. After all, Blake had never run into anything quite like Meghan before. That alone was enough to warp his judgement.

And yet, logically, she could give no reason for backing out. By all the standard guides, linking the new perfume with the world's most famous face made sense.

Eventually Gianna gave up, signed the contracts, and hoped that Meghan's busy schedule would put off any work on the ad campaign until Blake had a chance to return to his normal self.

But even that hope was taken away from her on a cold winter day just before Christmas. Blake tapped three times on the wall between their offices, and when she signalled for him to come in, he burst into her office with a portfolio full of ad layouts and spread them out on her desk. They were mere sketches of ideas, instructions for the photographers to follow, but the artist must have spent hours on his loving portrayal of Meghan, bringing her to life in the pencil sketches. The angular lines of the face, the big eyes, the classic nose, were unmistakable.

He had pictured Meghan, in negligee, with a crystal bottle of perfume in her hand. Meghan, at a restaurant table loaded with glitter, opening a box to show the crystal bottle. Meghan, in a bright tartan coat under a brilliant sky, putting a secret spray behind a tiny ear . . .

Always there was a man in the background. A handsome man, slightly out of focus, according to the instructions on the layout. And always the slogan——
Now every woman can be Sensually Meghan . . .

'What do you think?' asked Blake.

Gianna shrugged. 'It's all right. I've seen better.'

'I think it's darned good, considering they've had only ten days to work it up.'

'So what's the hurry? I'm sure it will be a while before Meghan can work us into her schedule.'

'That's the beauty of it, Gianna. We can start shooting right after New Year.' He sounded as eager as a child.

'Have you checked that out with Curtis?'

'Sure. Meghan happens to have about a week free. A project they'd planned fell through, so we can have the time. We'll have to shoot fast, of course, to have a whole campaign done in just a week, but we can do it. Gianna, we could have the product on the market by the end of January!'

'Have you forgotten the kind of lead time that magazine ads require, Blake?' asked Gianna.

'Of course not. But we can start with a television blitz, then follow up with the magazines. Besides, we've already bought magazine space months ahead, and just as soon as we have the new ads, we can substitute them for the old copy.'

'Dreamer!' she accused.

'I've checked it out, Gianna, and most of the magazines will let us do it. For an extra fee, of course.'

'That goes without saying.' She looked up with

concern in her eyes. 'Why are you in such a hurry, Blake?'

'Pure business sense. The sooner the product is out, the less likely that someone else will beat us to the idea.'

'But we really planned it for a spring release, or maybe even summer. It's crazy to put a perfume out in January, Blake! We've missed the Christmas rush, and it will be old hat by next year——'

Blake shrugged. 'So we'll pick up the Valentine's Day market instead.'

Gianna sighed. When he got in this frame of mind, there was no arguing with him.

'The agency has a terrific idea for later in the spring, too,' he went on. 'They want to take Meghan around the country to shoot the open-air scenes—with famous landmarks.'

'You must be joking! That will cost the earth, Blake.'

'It'll certainly be eye-catching.' He sprawled out in the comfortable chair beside her desk.

'Let's see how she does at attracting a market first.' I don't believe it, she thought. I'm supposed to be the one with the wacky ideas, and Blake's job is to keep me from jumping the track. I don't like this new arrangement at all.

'If there's time, we'll do one set during this first shooting session,' Blake added. 'Just to see how it looks.'

'We?'

'I think we should be there to observe. Someone has to make sure it meets our standards.'

'Let me know where to forward your mail,' Gianna said tartly.

He looked startled. 'What's eating you?'

'Nothing that you can fix,' she said.

He sat up. 'What happened to your enthusiasm?'

'Someone has to maintain some business sense around here. It seems that you've scarcely been around for the last two weeks, Blake.'

'Well, I have been spending a little time with Meghan—talking about the ad campaign——'

'Strictly business, hmm? If you say so, Blake. Just how much time have you spent with her?'

Blake shifted uncomfortably in his chair. 'Come on, Gianna——'

'How much time?' she persisted. 'Every evening?'

'Just about.'

She didn't even answer. 'Are you at least going to be at your parents' house for dinner tonight?' she persisted.

'Why? Are they expecting me?'

'Blake, I was in your office last week when your mother called to invite you.'

'Oh—I'd forgotten. I'm not sure if I'll go, Gianna. If I don't make it, tell her I'm working late, all right?'

Gianna uttered a frustrated little groan. 'With Meghan?'

He grinned, undisturbed by the sarcasm in her voice. 'Could be.'

'Well, if she doesn't get done shooting in time to go out with you, remember that your mother would be delighted to see you. I'm leaving now, so if you'd like to rhapsodise about Meghan, you'll have to do so at some other time.' She put her coat on.

'I wasn't rhapsodising. I was only telling you about the ads,' he said with dignity.

'I haven't time to argue, Blake,' she told him. 'I'm going to the airport to meet my parents.'

'Is that what the invitation was about?'

Gianna picked up a stapler and considered hitting him with it. 'Just in case you've forgotten,' she reminded him coldly, 'Christmas is the day after tomorrow. You are planning to come?'

'Tell John and Carol Hi for me.' He gathered the ad layouts together, and stood there looking at the top one with a smile.

Gianna exercised every ounce of restraint she could

muster, put the stapler down and left.

She was furious about it, all the way to O'Hare. The silly goon, she thought. He doesn't even have to have the real woman in front of him—he can go all soft and sentimental over a pencil sketch of her! What had happened to the sensible, practical big brother of her childhood?

Well, you asked for it, she reminded herself. You told him he should think about falling in love.

But I didn't mean he should pick someone like Meghan, she argued. I meant someone a little more ordinary, someone with a bit of common sense to her name. Someone who can appreciate him, and yet still see his flaws. That worshipful stare of Meghan's might be flattering now, but he'd tire of it some day. Or it would vanish, when Meghan realised that he wasn't a knight in shining armour after all. And what would that do to Blake?

'Dammit, he'll be miserable,' Gianna muttered. 'And I hate it when Blake's miserable.'

She was at the airport early; actually, she had planned to work another hour before leaving the office, but the ad copy and Blake's inanities had been the last straw in a frustrating day. She paced the crowded concourse, full of holiday travellers, and waited, and by the time her parents' plane was announced she had calmed down.

She had been overreacting, she decided. Blake was right about a few things. It had been crazy of her to want to back out of what might be the biggest deal of the century. Fear of failure can do funny things, she thought.

And he was even right about the out-of-town shooting sessions, she concluded. The new perfume was a good product, and with Meghan's name attached, it couldn't help but do well. Why shouldn't they spend some of the profits to make the ad campaign unique and draw even more attention to the product? They might have one of the champion sellers of all times on their hands, if they only promoted it right.

And perhaps Blake had been telling the truth when he said he'd been only talking business with Meghan, persuading her and soothing her ego. After all, what would a woman like Meghan—a famous, rich and glamorous woman like Meghan—see in Blake? He was a nice guy, but he'd said himself that there was really nothing about him to make a woman like Meghan sit up and notice. Meghan must treat every man like that, Gianna decided. Especially the men who were in a position to bring work her way. That was all.

And, feeling much better about the whole situation, she loooked up and spotted her parents.

It had been six months since she had seen them, and Gianna studied them carefully as they threaded their way through the bustling crowds towards her. They looked a little older, she thought, but wonderful. Her father's face was tanned, under his silver hair, from mornings on the golf course; Carol's skin was as soft and unwrinkled as Gianna rememberd it from childhood.

She held out her arms to her mother, and buried her face in the fox fur of Carol's jacket. It felt so good to be back in that soothing embrace!

'Hello, darling,' her father beamed, stooping to kiss her cheek. 'No snow? You promised snow.'

'It's forecast. And you don't escape without a hug, Daddy.'

He grinned and put his arms around her. 'Is that what you thought I was trying to do? I just wanted to get out of this crowd in a hurry.'

When they reached the car, John West lifted the luggage in, raising an eyebrow at the suitcase that was already in the boot. 'What's this?' he asked. 'Are you running away from home?'

Sometimes I'd like to, thought Gianna, then added, how odd—I've never felt that way before. I like it at the Whittaker house! 'Remember? You're the one who invited me to come along.'

He sighed. 'I suppose that means you women will turn Christmas into one gigantic slumber party!'

'That's all right, dear,' Carol told him. 'We'll let you do the slumbering for all of us.'

'We'll fix you women,' he threatened. 'Hal and Blake and I will kick the females out of the dining-room after dinner tonight, and we'll sit and drink port and smoke cigars till the wee hours. That'll show you!'

'John,' his wife reminded him, 'you never did like port, and you stopped smoking ten years ago.'

'Well, we'll think of something,' John said unrepentantly.

'Blake may not be there tonight, anyway,' said Gianna.

The sudden silence couldn't have been any sharper if she had announced that Christmas had been cancelled. She negotiated the heavy traffic with care, wondering if there was any way to explain Blake's defection without putting her foot further in her mouth. Regretfully, she finally decided there wasn't, short of telling them about Meghan, and that would only call for more explanations of things that were really none of their business. It left her feeling a little less than charitable towards Blake.

Blake had never missed an important family occasion before; Gianna didn't blame her parents for feeling a little left out if he didn't make the effort to greet them this time. After all, he was almost like a son to them. That's Meghan's influence, Gianna thought. She's turning him into an inconsiderate snob.

'That's a disappointment,' said Carol. 'You'll be dreadfully outnumbered without him, Gianna. You'll have to cope with the elderly set all by yourself——'

Before Gianna had a chance to bite her tongue, she had snapped, 'Don't worry about me! Since when was Blake any help?' She caught herself, and added, 'You're not elderly, anyway, and you're a lot of fun. I'd rather hang around with you and the Whittakers than anybody else I know.'

'What a charming daughter we have,' Carol murmured to John.

'And didn't we do a good job of raising her?' John replied, with mock humility. He reached across the back of the seat and shook his wife's hand. 'You should be commended, Mrs West.'

'And you, Mr West.'

'All right,' Gianna announced. 'Cut the nonsense, or I'll dump you right here and make you call a cab!'

'And she shows such respect for her elders, too,' Carol added.

Suddenly serious, Gianna said, 'Look, Blake and I are grown up now, you know. We both have other interests——' This wasn't going very well, she told herself. 'He'll be there for Christmas, I'm sure——'

Or was she sure? He hadn't said he would. What if he chose to spend Christmas with Meghan instead? What if Blake didn't bother to show up at all?

Oh, come on, Gianna, she told herself crossly. You can't believe he's that serious! And Meghan—surely Meghan has other plans. And yet here it was a mere two days before the holiday; if Meghan was going somewhere she'd have gone. But she was still in Chicago.

If Blake doesn't show up, she thought, and if he leaves me to explain to his parents and mine why he isn't coming, I'll simply die of embarrassment. After all, Blake's the one who says that the four of them cherish fond hopes for our future——

Was that, perhaps, why he was acting this way? Was this his way of announcing to the assembled parents that there was no future for their hopes?

Well, he could at least come out in the open with it, she thought, instead of hiding behind me this way. He could at least face up to it like a man, and bring Meghan out to meet his parents——

He might even have invited Meghan for Christmas. He hadn't said anything that ruled out the possibility. If he brings that woman here for the holiday without warning me first, Gianna decided, I'll kill him on the spot! And then I'll die of embarrassment.

The thought of Meghan, once entertained, did not disappear easily. Blake just might bring her out to Oak Park, Gianna knew. And if he did, why should he feel it necessary to tell Gianna ahead of time? She already knew how he felt; he'd certainly made no effort to keep his attraction to Meghan quiet.

Well, Gianna decided, I just hope he has the decency to warn his mother!

The smell of Christmas was heavy in the Whittaker house. The sharp scent of pine garlands mingled with the tingly aromas of nutmeg and cinnamon and peppermint extract. The tree was already lighted, its branches heavy with glistening ornaments, the angel on the topmost branch brushing against the ceiling of the formal living-room. Tinsel swayed and shivered and glistened at each tiny movement of the air.

The punchbowl on the sideboard was full of eggnog, and Hal Whittaker liberally dispensed glasses along with hugs in the flurry of greetings. Gianna stood off to the side and watched, amused, as the four old friends disposed of the long separation in a matter of minutes.

Gwen clucked anxiously about how thin Carol was getting, admired John's tan, and shepherded Hal off upstairs with the luggage. 'John and Carol have the guest-room,' she announced. 'Gianna, you'll be in Blake's old room.'

It hit Gianna with the force of a blow. Did that mean that Blake had told his mother he wasn't coming at all?

'Blake will have to make do with the fold-out couch in my sewing-room,' Gwen went on comfortably. 'It will serve him right for being the last one here. More eggnog, anyone?'

Gianna listened to the cheerful talk for a while, then excused herself, feeling she had to have a moment by herself. She let herself quietly into the room that had been Blake's and lifted her bag on to one of the twin beds to start listlessly unpacking. She carried a handful of clothes to the closet and stopped by a wall shelf full of rocks, each neatly labelled in Blake's schoolboy handwriting. She picked up a geode, the smooth, worn shell broken open to display the gleam of crystals within. Rock collecting was only one of the many projects he had pursued. Gwen still kept the things dusted, she realised.

It was obvious, Gianna thought, that Gwen knew nothing about Meghan. If Blake put a wrench in the works by bringing Meghan——

'Oh, stop it!' she told herself irritably. The worst that could happen would be that Blake would be caught in an embarrassing position. That had nothing to do with Gianna; in fact, she would find it rather humorous.

Except for one thing, she realised uneasily. Gwen's house was now full of company. She looked across the room at the twin beds with foreboding. If Blake brought Meghan home, she realised, she would end up sharing a bedroom with the world's most famous model.

'That kind of competition isn't fair,' she muttered, then drew herself up short. After all, she reminded herself, who did she think was competing? And for what? Blake?

'That,' she told herself firmly, 'is a joke.'

The big drawing-room was dusky, lit only by the hundreds of twinkling coloured bulbs on the tree and by the embers of a blaze in the huge fireplace. Outside, the promised snow fell gently from a heavy sky, bringing a blanket of silence to a softened world. It was Christmas Eve, and they had just finished off an enormous tureen of clam chowder. By tradition, Christmas Eve supper was supposed to be a light meal, but the half-dozen homemade breads and three varieties of desserts had tempted them all, and Gianna dropped to the carpet in front of the hearth with a groan.

'If you have a stomach ache,' Blake told her unsympathetically, 'you have only yourself to blame.' He put another log on the fire and stretched out on the hearthrug beside her, on his stomach, to watch the flames grow.

'On the contrary,' Gianna argued, 'it's your mother's fault. She didn't have to tell me she'd made cheesecake for dessert.' She pulled her knees up under her chin and clasped her arms around them, watching the fire. It was pleasant here, in this quiet room, surrounded by the people who meant the most in the world to her. And, Mhe added, without Meghan to complicate things.

Blake had turned up, the night before, windblown and red-cheeked from the cold, but alone, thank heaven—as Gianna had found herself thinking gratefully—in time for after-dinner coffee. She had manged a private word with him late in the evening, and was told that Meghan had departed via a late flight for home.

'Where's she going?' she had asked.

Blake had frowned. 'I'm not supposed to tell,' he said, 'It's only a little town, and she likes to protect her privacy——'

Gianna had stuck her tongue out at him childishly. 'What do you think I'm going to do?' she had asked. 'Call up the news media?' Not that she had really cared where Meghan had gone, she thought now, as long as she wasn't in Oak Park, intruding on this warm family celebration. 'I thought you might bring her along.' She was proud of the easy tone of her voice.

Blake shrugged. 'I didn't think Mom and Dad were quite ready for the shock,' he admitted.

It had stopped Gianna in her tracks. So he was as serious as that, was he?

But after that brief exchange, Meghan had not been

mentioned again. It was almost as if the model had vanished entirely, memories and all. Blake had spent the day teasing Gianna unmercifully, as if they had both been teenagers again. Just as if, she thought, nothing had changed at all. And yet, underneath, she couldn't quite dismiss the nagging thought that nothing would ever be quite the same again.

Across the room, Gwen and Carol were huddled together on a couch, giggling as they turned the pages of a brittle old book. 'Listen to this!' Carol cried. 'It's from thirty years ago, and it's a masterpiece of understatement. 'Christmas is not very exciting to a baby who's just over three weeks old——'

'Oh, not this again!' muttered Blake.

'Why not?' asked Gianna. 'It's tradition to look back on past holidays.'

'You wouldn't say that if it was you they were talking about. It's embarrassing.'

'Blake, have a heart! They haven't been together on Christmas Eve in five years. Let them have fun.'

'Wait till they start reading bits about you out of there. I can't wait for the Christmas where you got your first pantyhose. What a hoot!'

The Christmas album had been around far longer than either Blake or Gianna could remember. It was only brought out on Christmas Eve, when the entries of years past were read, reviving memories of holidays long vanished. Then, after the new holiday was over, a few brief paragraphs were written about it, the photographs were captioned, and the year's greeting cards and letters were glued in place. Then the book was folded away in tissue paper for another year.

'"Blake slept through both Santa Claus and Christmas dinner, to the great disappointment of his parents,"' Carol went on.

'You were a stick-in-the-mud even when you were three weeks old!' laughed Gianna, on a note of discovery.

'As I recall,' he challenged, 'your father spent your first Christmas dinner in the bathroom with the shower running, because you had the croup. So there!'

Gianna shrugged. 'At least I kept things lively. And how would you know, anyway? You would have been only two yourself.'

'I will never forget the awful noises you used to make.'

Gwen looked up with a smile. 'Blake, do you remember being disappointed when Gianna turned out to be a girl?'

'Was I really?' He sounded fascinated. 'I had good taste even then.'

Gianna punched him in the arm.

'You certainly seemed to think it was inconsiderate of Carol not to have produced a boy to be your playmate,' his mother went on.

'Before she was born, you used to sit on my lap and talk to her,' Carol added, and turned the page of the Christmas album. 'You'd even decided on a name.'

'Who was I going to be?' asked Gianna, a little fearfully.

'Oh, we wouldn't have named you that, anyway,' her mother assured her. 'It would have been a dreadful thing to do to a baby, even if you had been a boy. I only mention it to illustrate the possessive attitude Blake had at the time—he seemed to think he owned you.'

'And I'll bet,' Blake put in, 'that by the time she was walking, I was ready to sell her.' He stretched, and sat up. 'I think I'll go for a walk in the snow.'

'What's the matter?' Gianna gibed. 'Is the reminiscence level getting a little steep for you?'

'Of course not. But just to even things out, what about the Christmas you came down with chickenpox?' asked Blake. 'You came to the dinner-table in your pyjamas, and I ended up quarantined, too!'

'That reminds me,' Carol said, 'there's a box under the

tree, Gianna, wrapped in bright red foil. It's to be opened tonight.'

Gianna probed under the tree and located a large rectangular box with her name on the tag.

'Do I get to open a package early, too?' asked Blake.

Gwen dropped easily into the motherly tone of long-gone years. 'Of course not,' she said. 'Gianna is younger, so she gets a few extra privileges at Christmas time.'

'It's only pyjamas, anyway,' Gianna muttered. 'I don't know why you're so excited about it. Mother, don't you think I'm getting a little old for this?'

'It's tradition, honey.'

'I know. I've got new pyjamas every Christmas Eve since I can remember, but I am twenty-eight years old now——'

'Gianna, you wouldn't rob me of my fun, would you?' There was a gleam of humour in her mother's eyes.

Gianna looked at Carol, then down at the bright box in her lap. Just what was the woman up to now? she wondered, with slight foreboding.

Surely her mother wouldn't have put anything embarrassing in here, and asked her to open it in public! But what if she opened this box to find a satin nightgown, or a lacy teddy, or a sheer bikini sleep set? Just what kind of a statement was her mother trying to make, anyway?

'Come on,' Blake urged. 'Rip it open. You're the one who can't stand to open a package slowly.'

'I'm scared to death of this one,' Gianna muttered. But there was no escaping it, So she tore the foil paper to shreds. The box carried the name of a premier store. Gianna had shopped there on her last trip to Florida, but all she could remember now was the huge lingerie section, racks and racks of sexy nightwear and under-things. She had a vague memory of stopping here and there among the frilly garments to exclaim. Good grief, she thought, what on earth did I say about those things that might have made Mother think I wanted to own them?

She lifted the lid carefully, as if afraid the contents might jump out at her. Released from confinement, the silver tissue paper billowed out, and she pulled it cautiously aside.

Instead of chiffon or satin or lace, though, her fingers stroked the softness of velour, and she started to giggle as she unfolded a forest green pyjama jumpsuit, made almost like a baby's snowsuit, complete with feet. It zipped up the front, there was a hood to pull up over her ears, and there was even a teddy-bear appliqué on the pocket.

'Where on earth did you get this?' she demanded. 'And why?'

Carol laughed. 'You did say the heat had gone off in your apartment, the last time we talked to you,' she reminded her.

'And you didn't want your baby to be cold? Thanks, Mom, that's sweet.'

'Are you going to model it?' asked Blake.

'Only in the privacy of my own bedroom.' But Gianna's hand stroked the soft velour.

'Suit yourself,' Blake shrugged. 'But it looks more comfortable than what you're wearing.'

Her wool slacks were a little scratchy, she decided. And her jacket was binding. The pyjama suit was certainly less revealing than many of the outfits she wore all summer. Why not? she thought, and jumped up.

As she left the room, she heard her father say, 'Speaking of bedrooms—some sleep sounds like a mighty good idea.'

When Gianna came back to the living-room a few minutes later it was silent except for the hiss of the dying fire. She thought for an instant that everyone had gone to bed, until Blake looked up from the hearthrug and remarked, 'That thing makes you look like an unripe pumpkin.'

'Gee, thanks!'

'The compliments are free. Come on down. I'll even share my pillow.'

Gianna dropped to the carpet beside him. 'What happened to everybody?' she asked.

'They seem to have concluded that we need our privacy.'

'For what?'

Blake shrugged. 'Why don't you stop asking questions and just enjoy the fire?'

She stretched out beside him, where the warmth of the flames could caress her face. 'I thought you were going for a walk.'

'I looked out at the snow and decided the sidewalks are too slippery.'

'I'm glad,' she murmured.

'That the sidewalks are slippery?'

'No, silly—that you didn't go. I was afraid you'd have an accident.' She settled her cheek comfortably into the pillow.

The grandfather clock in the hall gathered its strength with a little whir, and began to chime midnight. Gianna raised up on an elbow to listen to it, and looked down at Blake. A feeling of warmth and serenity swept over her.

'It's nice to be together again at Christmas, isn't it?' she murmured. 'All of us together.'

'Very nice,' he said softly.

'Merry Christmas, Blake,' she whispered, and bent her head to drop a kiss on his cheek.

At least her intention was to give him a gentle kiss on the cheek. But at that instant, Blake turned his head, and her lips brushed his instead.

The contact was like fire racing through her veins. Her throat seemed to close tight. She wanted to pull away, but something wouldn't let her move. The effort to breathe hurt her lungs.

This is insane, she thought. You've kissed him before, and it was no big deal. He's like a big brother, for

heaven's sake! This is nothing to write home about——
But this wasn't like kissing a brother.

She looked down at him and tried to laugh it off.
'Sorry,' she said. 'It was a wonderful idea, just
misdirected——'

He didn't answer. His eyes were dark; in the dimness
of the room, she couldn't tell if he was angry or on the
brink of laughter. In the fireplace, a log popped and a
flame burst forth, sending shadows wavering across the
ceiling. Blake's hand crept up from the carpet, over the
soft velour pyjamas and to the nape of her neck, and
pulled her down to him.

'Blake——' Her voice was panicky. But there was no
time for any more of a protest than that, before he was
kissing her again.

There was nothing accidental about this caress.
Slowly, deliberately, his mouth moved aginst hers,
tasting, sampling this new sensation. Gianna stopped
breathing.

In a long and varied dating career, she had never been
kissed quite like this before. It felt as if her blood had
turned to crystals that pricked each cell with tiny stabs of
delight. For that first long moment, she was aware of
nothing except the insane reaction of her own body, and
of the warmth of his mouth caressing her.

He murmured her name, and pulled her down till she
was so close against him that when he drew a breath it
seemed to suffice for both of them. She wanted to mould
herself to the hardness of his muscled body, to allow
herself to become a part of him——

Then she remembered that she was lying on the
hearthrug, kissing a man she had never considered as
anything other than a brother—and allowing him to
touch her, to hold her, to treat her as a lover would.

She broke away from him as if his body had suddenly
scorched her, and sat up, the back of her hand pressed
hard against her mouth, breathing in gasps as if to make

up for the oxygen she had been unable to absorb before.

Blake put a gentle hand on her shoulder. 'Gianna——'

But she jerked away from the warmth of his fingers against the soft velour. 'How could you?' she accused, her voice raspy and harsh. She was fighting to hold back the tears, but she was losing the battle. She wiped her face with trembling fingers, stumbled to her feet, and ran up the stairs to the sanctuary of her room.

'Blake,' she whispered to herself, as she closed the door and leaned against it. 'How could you do this to me?'

And just who, she wondered suddenly, had taught him to kiss like that? Meghan? 'There's certainly nothing wrong with that technique,' she muttered, and wiped furiously at the tears again.

CHAPTER SIX

GIANNA stood by the door for a long time, trying to convince herself that she was all right, that nothing important had happened down there by the fire. But it was important, her heart screamed, and no amount of talking would make the reality go away.

She had been betrayed. The boy who had taught her to fly a kite, the big brother who had protected her from the school bullies, the young man who had listened to her confidences and never repeated what she had told him, the business partner who sometimes disagreed but who always respected her opinion—all of them had vanished in the few seconds that burning kiss had lasted. Instead, a stranger had been there beside her on the hearthrug—a man she had never seen before, and one she had no desire to know better.

'Blake,' she said to the empty room, and it was a mournful cry for the trusted friend who had violated her faith in him.

She didn't know how long she stood there, huddled against the door. Eventually, exhausted from the weight of tears, she climbed into bed and lay rigid in the dark, painfully aware of Blake's things around her. Even the rock collection on the wall shelf seemed to jeer at her, to sneer that she thought she knew him, and yet she had known so little at all.

When a cautious tap sounded at the door, she jerked upright in shock. Then she padded soft-footed across the room and leaned against the panel. 'Go away, Blake!' she whispered fiercely.

There was a brief silence. 'Damn it, Gianna, it was only a kiss!' he growled.

She held her breath and didn't answer, and a few moments later, with a muttered curse, he went away.

Gianna crept back to her bed, and cried a little more.

By morning, however, sanity had reasserted itself. How foolish could she be? she asked herself. He was right; it had only been a kiss. One kiss, and she had concluded that he had mad designs on her virtue! Blake was probably as embarrassed this morning as she was, she concluded. She owed him an apology, and if she had been anything but a nitwit, she would have made it when he came to her door last night, instead of making a Broadway production out of it.

It wasn't too late for the apology, at least, she thought, and got dressed in a hurry, hoping to catch him before the entire family assembled. She had heard no noises this morning from the sewing-room, just next to the room she was using. Perhaps Blake was still in bed.

She made sure the hallway was empty before she tapped at his door. It was embarrassing enough to be doing this at all, she thought, but for one of their parents to see her sneaking into Blake's bedroom would be worse.

'Though,' she muttered, 'any one of the four of them would probably wish me a pleasant Merry Christmas and go on downstairs to tell the rest that we'll be very late to breakfast, without turning a hair!'

There was no answer to her knock. She waited a moment, then pushed the door cautiously open. The sewing-room was empty, the bed folded neatly back into the couch as if it had never been used. Blake was nowhere to be seen.

Downstairs, the Whittakers and the Wests were gathered in the dining room, drinking a second cup of coffee, but there was no sign of Blake.

Had he left the house altogether? Gianna asked herself uneasily. Now that's the most ridiculous idea of all, she thought. He wouldn't do that at Christmas; it would upset his mother and cause all kinds of questions. But she couldn't shake the fear.

'Good morning, dear,' said Gwen. 'I hope you slept well. Blake's bringing in some warm croissants, I believe.'

Gianna's eyes went automatically to the swinging door that led to the kitchen. 'I'll see if he needs help.' she said, and fled before anyone could question why Blake might not be capable of carrying a basket of rolls by himself.

He was taking a plate of tiny sausages out of the microwave, and he looked up with a quizzical expression, one eyebrow raised. Before she could find the words she needed, he said, 'I hope you're not planning to continue the scene you started last night.'

Gianna's jaw dropped. Her intention of apologising vanished. 'What do you mean, the scene *I* started?'

'You know perfectly well what I'm referring to,' Blake said impatiently. 'You went flying out of the room like an offended virgin, and I'm not going to stand for you acting high-and-mighty about it today.'

'Oh, you aren't?' she asked sweetly.

'No. I won't allow everyone's holiday to be ruined because you got a reaction you didn't expect last night.'

'You make it sound as if I asked for that kind of treatment!'

'Didn't you? You were the one who came downstairs in pyjamas, and snuggled up next to the fire——'

'That doesn't excuse what you did, Blake!'

'Dammit, Gianna, I didn't drag you off to my cave by the hair! It was only a kiss!'

She turned her back on him. Her hands were trembling just a little as she rearranged the warm rolls in the basket and carefully folded the linen napkin around them. Her pride had been stung by his attack; she was darned if she'd apologise to him now!

'That's right, Blake,' she said. 'It was only a kiss. There was nothing special about it at all. I can't think why it upset me, unless it was because I was offended at your poor technique.' She sneaked a look up at him through her eyelashes, and was delighted to see that he looked furious.

'In future,' she concluded, 'Whenever you feel the need for practice—call Meghan, and leave me out of it.'

'At least Meghan isn't a shrew,' snapped Blake. 'And she doesn't come to pieces and treat a man to hysterics whenever she's touched!'

'Oh, we all agree Meghan is perfect. The only question remaining is, what does the perfect woman see in you, Blake Whittaker?' Gianna picked up the basket of croissants and marched into the dining room, leaving a startled Blake behind.

But the momentary victory wasn't worth the price.

Half a dozen times on that Christmas Day she had forgotten about their quarrel and turned to Blake to make a humorous comment or share the kind of pained glance they had often exchanged when one of their parents said something particularly odd. But suddenly, Blake no longer seemed to share the joke. Once he looked at her as if she had lost her mind; the rest of the time he seemed to be absorbed in something across the room, and completely unaware of Gianna.

She opened her packages and made the appropriate exclamations, but she hardly saw what was in each box. The only exception was the crystal apple, carefully packed in a velvet-lined case, that Blake had given her.

Gianna looked down at the flawless thing, its perfect clarity cupped in her hands, then raised her head with tears in her eyes. 'It's beautiful,' she said softly, 'Thank you, Blake.'

He shrugged off the comment. 'Now at least you'll never run out of apples,' he said.

And it had been the last civil comment he had addressed to her all day, too, she reflected. In fact, it had been the last time he'd had anything pleasant to say to her for the greater part of a week.

The Christmas spirit had not extended past the four walls of the Whittaker house. Once they were back at work, the silence had deepened. More than once, Gianna had braced herself to apologise for the sharp remarks she had made on Christmas morning, but so far Blake had given her no opportunity to make up. As far as he was concerned, it seemed to Gianna, nothing she could say would make any difference—and so he refused to listen to her at all.

She looked down at the apple, cupped in her hands like a crystal ball, then put it carefully back in the box on the corner of her desk. Part of her wanted to cry. It was a gift she would never have expected from Blake. Hundreds of dollars' worth of crystal apple, good only to put on a shelf, hardly seemed like the practical Blake, except that Blake had always known just how to choose the things she would like the very best.

I can't stand it, she thought. I can't put up with this silence any more, this feeling that I'm working with a stranger! We have to do something to get over this mess we've created—and I'll have to be the one to do it, because Blake obviously isn't going to.

She did still owe him an apology, that was for sure. No matter what he'd done, she had been the one who had turned an incident into a production. She'd start with that, she thought with sudden determination. And if he still didn't want to listen to her—well, she would make him listen, that was all.

She burst into his office, and was greeted with a frown. He cupped his hand over the mouthpiece of the telephone and said, 'Is this something that can wait, Gianna?'

'Of course,' she mumbled. 'I'll come back when you're free.' She retreated, and saw that their secretary was watching her, open-mouthed. It was painfully obvious that the woman had overhead Blake's comment, and it was just as apparent that she had never heard that tone of voice from Blake in the office before.

At least you could have been smart enough to tap on the door, Gianna berated herself. Or use the jungle intercom to find out if he was busy. But no, you had to go sailing in there to make an apology, and before you could even say a word, you succeeded in making him angrier still . . .

It was nearly half an hour later when Blake came into her office. He didn't knock, she noticed irritably.

'What is it, Gianna?' he asked. There was a brisk tone to his voice, as if he was eager to have her problem disposed of. He sat down on the edge of her desk.

She looked up at him with annoyance. He hadn't sat on her desk in years; he was doing it now, she was sure, only because he knew how much the habit irritated her. That, and because it put her at a disadvantage, having to look so far up to meet his eyes.

'Well, Gianna?' he said. 'I do have work to do.'

She almost said, then go do it, before Meghan comes back and no work gets done at all! But she thought better of it, and strangled the impulse.

'My parents are leaving this afternoon,' she said instead.

'I know.'

'I think they'd like it if you'd come with me to see them off at the airport.'

'Why?'

She gave an impatient little sigh. 'Blake, you've scarcely seen them all week. You went back to your apartment the day after Christmas, instead of staying with your parents——'

'For obvious reasons,' he interrupted. 'Have you ever tried sleeping on the fold-out bed in Mom's sewing-room?'

'Please, Blake. It would really mean a lot to them——'

'Wouldn't it just be building up their hopes?'

'For us getting married, you meanH Blake, I'm not asking you to pretend to be engaged!' she protested.

'No,' he agreed. 'I understand that; being engaged might mean that you'd have to kiss me a time or two, and heaven knows the trouble you'd have with that!'

Gianna took a deep breath and controlled her temper with an effort. 'There's no need to be sarcastic,' she said. 'I want to apologise for what happened—for what I said and everything.'

'You don't know what came over you,' Blake said coldly. There was the barest hint of sarcasm in his voice.

'That's not quite the way I'd have put it, but——' suddenly, the longing to have things fixed was more than she could bear. She put an impulsive hand on his sleeve. 'Blake, can't we just forget that kiss ever happened? I want things to be back to normal!'

He raised an eyebrow. 'By normal, you mean—what?'

'We were best friends. I want that back, Blake. I want things to be the way they used to be!'

'You want to be pals,' he said. There was an odd twist to his words.

'Yes,' she said eagerly, happy that he understood. 'It would be a sin for us to lose that, because of one stupid kiss!'

There was a brief silence. Then Blake sighed. 'I'll come to O'Hare with you this afternoon.'

Gianna rewarded him with a smile. 'Mother and Dad will be so glad. They're fond of you, you know.'

'Yes,' Blake said drily, 'I know. If that's all, I have work to do.'

'Blake——'

He turned at the door.

'I'm glad we got this worked out,' she said softly. 'I— I've missed you.'

He didn't answer. The door clicked shut behind him.

With a sigh of relief, Gianna turned to her own work. It was more fun now, she thought, now that the problem with Blake was solved.

The holiday travelling rush was still heavy, and Gianna and her mother walked on ahead while John and Blake took care of the luggage. 'This is crazy,' laughed Carol. 'We're going back with twice as much stuff as we brought. So much for the wonderful resolution not to tie ourselves down with possessions any more!'

'Did you find some bargains?' asked Gianna.

'Darling, you wouldn't believe it! Gwen and I went downtown yesterday, to take advantage of the after-Christmas sales. I've never seen so many people in the Loop. But bargains——Oh, I do miss Chicago so much, Gianna!'

'Even with the cold?'

Carol sighed. 'Even that, I'm afraid. You don't really appreciate nice weather until you've had some bracing wind.'

'That's a different outlook,' Gianna mused.

'But of course it's the people that I really miss,' Carol said. 'You'd think, as long as I've been in Florida, that I would have made one friend as close as Gwen. But——' She broke off, and giggled. 'You'll never believe what we did this morning.'

'I'm afraid to guess,' smiled Gianna ruefully.

'We called a real-estate agent, and went house-hunting!'

Gianna's mouth was open. 'You're thinking of moving back here?'

'No, of course not. But Gwen said she'd heard our old house was on the market, and I just had to see it again, Gianna.'

'You actually pretended to be interested in buying our old house back?'

'Well, I didn't have to pretend very hard,' Carol pointed out. 'Mr Elliot—the real-estate man—didn't ask any questions. And after all, I did want to see what the new owners had done to it.'

'And?' Gianna prompted. 'You can't just leave me up in the air like that, Mom!'

'It's really not bad. The new wallpaper is awful, of course—all Art Deco. There isn't anything that's in really bad taste, but it just doesn't seem to fit in the house. And she's put a patterned foil in the dining room——' Carol shivered artistically. 'It has butterflies on it—huge butterflies. But it's obvious that they've taken good care of the house.'

'Why are they selling it?' asked Gianna.

'His company is transferring him to the West Coast. I feel very sorry for them, actually; I know how hard it is to leave that house. You should go look at it, Gianna.'

Gianna shook her head. 'I think I'd rather remember it as it was.'

'I hadn't thought of that. You always looked at it differently from how your father and I did, I suppose. For us, it was just a house.'

Gianna nodded. 'I don't really remember any of the other houses we lived in,' she said. 'That one was always home to me.'

'Then perhaps you're right in thinking it would be better to stay away,' Carol said. 'I suppose we'll have to say goodbye here. Look at those crowds!'

'I wish you could stay longer.' Gianna's voice was threatening to crack.

'It's probably just as well,' her mother said lightly. 'My credit limit wouldn't have lasted another three days.'

Bless my mother, Gianna thought. She knows I'm about to cry, and she refuses to make it harder for me. She hugged Carol hard.

'Goodness, child, I'll have cracked ribs if you keep that up!' Carol protested. 'Blake, thank you for coming today.' She gave him a warm hug, and he kissed her cheek.

The men shook hands, then Gianna's father held out

his arms to her for a last embrace. 'Blake, take care of my little girl,' he said gruffly.

'Daddy,' she protested, her face buried in the shoulder of his coat, 'I can look out for myself!'

'Ah,' he said solemnly, 'but that's no fun, Gianna.' A moment more and they were gone.

Gianna watched them out of sight, and wiped a tear off her cheek. 'They are just a little obvious about it, aren't they?' she said, trying to keep her voice steady.

'Of course. They think they've found the perfect solution.'

'Well, I'm sure they'll survive the disappointment.'

Blake didn't comment. 'Are you going home now?'

'Sure. There's no point in me staying with your parents, when mine have gone home.' She pulled on her gloves as they walked towards the car park.

'Sometimes I think Mom would like to adopt you,' he mused.

'Maybe they should have traded us, years ago. Thanks for coming with me, Blake. It meant a lot to them, I know.'

He wasn't looking at her, and his voice was distant as he said, 'Any time youBXneed help saying goodbye to your parents at the airport, give me a call.'

Gianna laughed. 'Well, that's safe. You're not apt to be called on to keep that promise for a while, are you? Next Christmas, I'll probably go to Florida.'

It was only a little past five o'clock, but already the sky looked like midnight, and the gold street lights spread like a jewelled necklace over the city. The shortest day of the year had come and gone, but it would be a few weeks yet before the days were appreciably longer. This was the season she disliked the most, Gianna thought. She got up in the dark, drove to work in the almost-dark, came home in the dark.

The parking lot at Westway was nearly empty. The workers on the main production line had left earlier in the afternoon, when their shift was done. Now just the small number of swing shift workers remained in the factory. The office end of the building was almost deserted.

Gianna pulled her car into the spot next to where Blake had left his. She felt lonely already, she thought. She wasn't looking forward to that drive across Chicago, alone in the cold night, with an empty apartment as her destination. 'How about coming over for some gin rummy tonight?' she asked. 'I'll stop and get Chinese food.'

Blake shook his head. 'Not tonight, Gianna. I'm going to work late.'

'What's so important that you have to do it tonight?'

'This campaign for the new perfume.'

'I thought the ad agency had it all figured out.'

'Oh, they do, as far as the ads are concerned. We start shooting the day after New Year.'

Meghan would be back in two more days? Gianna sighed. 'I assumed she was taking a little time off,' she said.

'She's had a week.'

'My, aren't you generous?'

'I didn't set the schedule, Curtis did. He wants to get this campaign shot as quickly as possible, and by working over the weekend we can squeeze in some extra time.'

'He's probably afraid if she has too much time of, she'll start dreaming of banana splits,' Gianna said cattily. 'But if the ads are taken care of, what is there left to do?'

'The publicity. Meghan is news, right now, and if we can capitalise on that, it'll be more effective than buying ads.'

'What are you working on?'

'I called one of the talk-show hosts this afternoon, and we're scheduled for a show at the end of next week. You'd be amazed, Gianna, at how many reporters are dying for a chance to talk to Meghan.'

'All men, of course,' she said sweetly.

Blake shot a disapproving look at her. 'Not all of them, no. And it is a legitimate news story—famous model teams with famous cosmetics firm.'

'I do hope Curtis appreciates what you're doing for his client's career,' said Gianna, with soft malice in her voice.

'I'm doing it for the company,' Blake said. 'Any publicity that Meghan gets right now will be money in our pockets.'

'And of course, it can't hurt Meghan either.'

'It's sort of a fringe benefit for her.'

'Oh, of course,' she said, with gentle irony. 'Well, before you get too absorbed in the shooting, perhaps we can plan something for tomorrow. It is New Year's Eve, you know.'

Blake looked positively uncomfortable. 'I can't, Gianna.'

'Oh? Are you going to a party without me? For shame, Blake!' There was a teasing note in her voice, but a bit of disappointment lurked beneath it. They had always rung in the New Year together, since they'd been in school!

'Not a party, exactly,' he explained. 'I have a date.'

Gianna knew she should keep her mouth shut. Failing that, she even considered several replies, any of which would have been appropriate, in the circumstances. She could have politely said, I see; some other time, then. Or, Have a good time, Blake. Or, I'm delighted to see that you're getting out more.

Instead she heard herself say pettishly, 'Going out with Meghan a few times has really increased your confidence, hasn't it?'

'Well, you didn't seem to want to have anything to do with me.' Blake opened the car door, and a blast of wind swirled in, taking Giana's breath away.

She already knew that, but being reminded only made

her angrier at herself. She struck back at him. 'Didn't you hear me, Blake?' she asked. 'Who's the lucky girl?'

He turned and put his head back in the car. 'Meghan,' he said softly, and slammed the door.

Before she could gather her wits he was gone, striding up the sidewalk to the main door. 'Well!' Gianna muttered to herself, and put the car into gear.

After the warmth and light and laughter of the Whittaker house, her apartment was gloomy and chilly. She hadn't been home in a week, and dust had begun to collect. The tiny Christmas tree looked droopy and forlorn, and fully half its needles were embedded in the carpet. She felt less than enthusiastic about cleaning up the mess, but she remembered something her mother had told her long before; whenever she was feeling angry, Carol got out the cleaning supplies and took out her frustrations on the dirt.

There were worse ways to spend an evening, Gianna decided, and got the vacuum cleaner out of the closet. She didn't stop to wonder why she was feeling so frustrated.

I'll show him, she thought. I don't have to sit at home on New Year's Eve. There are plenty of men I can call.

And how many of them, she wondered, will be waiting for their phones to ring? Everybody plans ahead for New Year's Eve.

She could always call Rod. Their blind date a month or so before had gone well enough, except that he hadn't been able to remember that her name wasn't Gina. 'So who cares?' she asked herself wryly. 'Everyone has a fault here and there.' Except that it would be horrible if she called and he didn't even recognise her name! No, Rod was out.

Eric had told her that he'd be out of town. Craig had acquired a new girlfriend, Curtis—— She sighed.

Maybe she should give up on the idea of a date and just go to a party alone. She'd been invited to all her friends' holiday parties; an extra woman was always welcome there.

But I don't want to go to a party alone, she thought rebelliously. That isn't going to prove anything!

Dave, she thought. Good old Dave. He'd taken her out to dinner a couple of weeks earlier. Nice guy, good-looking and blond, an accountant for a tax firm in the Loop, and a gentleman. 'I wonder why he never called back,' she murmured. Funny that she hadn't even noticed till now.

She had been a little preoccupied over dinner that night, she remembered, concerned about how she was going to tell Blake that she didn't want to sign those contracts. Maybe it was no wonder Dave hadn't called back! She'd scarcely noticed him that night. Well, Dave it was. He might be surprised that she called, but at least he was too much of a gentleman to embarrass her.

Yes, she decided. As soon as she was finished cleaning, she'd call Dave and see if he wanted to go out tomorrow evening, or come over for popcorn or something.

Two hours later, the vacuum was still sprawled across the carpet, beside a paper bag full of accumulated dust and dirt. She'd managed to get the full bag removed, but the new one wouldn't go in right, and whenever she flipped the switch to turn the machine on, it started to blow clouds of dust around the room.

'I have to solve this myself,' she said firmly. 'I will not call Blake to fix it for me.' She took the new bag out, turned it over, put it back in. An experimental flick of the switch left her choking. 'Damn,' she said crossly, and started over.

The telephone rang. Maybe it's Blake, she thought, reconsidering the idea of Chinese food. 'If that's him,' she said with determination, 'I will not tell him about this.' She pushed the machine aside.

It was not Blake; it was Norman Brown. 'Gianna?' he asked hesitantly, 'Cluny's having a New Year's Eve party tomorrow night——'

'Seems like a reasonable choice of times,' Gianna muttered under her breath.

'What? I didn't quite hear you.'

'Nothing, Norman.'

'Oh.' He sounded confused, and there was a long silence.

'Did you call me up to give me the news? Or was there something else?' She was being nasty, she knew, and she bit her tongue. After all, it wasn't Norman's fault!

'I wondered if you'd be my date,' he ventured.

'Oh, Norman, I don't think Cluny would really appreciate having me there——'

'She's hosting it at a restaurant. She has a party room and everything.'

'Not the restaurant we went to for dinner that night, I hope.' Gianna's protest slipped out before she even thought about it.

'Oh, no. this is a really nice one.'

'Well, thank you for the invitation, Norman, but I doubt that Cluny would welcome my presence.'

'Well, it's my party, too,' he said. 'And you're really the only girl I know well enough to ask.'

How horribly flattering! Gianna thought.

'I'm sorry I couldn't ask you earlier. I suppose you have a dozen other things to do, don't you?'

He sounded like a beagle puppy would, if only the puppy could talk, Gianna thought. At least he had given her a good excuse; all she needed to do was to say that yes, she had other plans.

Plans to do what? she thought rebelliously. To stay home and wash my hair? Watch the late movie? Clean the apartment again? Call Dave? Don't kid yourself, she thought. He won't be there.

'I'd like to come with you, Norman,' she said.

'You would? You really would?'

Well, she thought, let's not push it. But I'm darned if

I'll stay at home just because Blake has other plans. I'm through with depending on Blake.

'Gee,' Norman said eagerly, 'wait till Cluny hears about this!'

Right, Gianna thought. I might be able to hear the explosion from here. She gave Norman her address, agreed to be ready at eight, and put the telephone down. Then she turned to the vacuum cleaner with new determination.

'All right, buster,' she warned it. 'There isn't going to be any more Blake around here. It's just you and me, now—and I warn you I don't give up easy.' She gave the bag a twist and a jerk, and turned the switch on.

It worked perfectly, and Giana stood in the centre of the carpet with her mouth open in astonishment. 'I'll be darned,' she said finally. 'I actually fixed it!'

Doing without Blake, she decided, was going to be a snap. She'd show him that she didn't need him after all!

CHAPTER SEVEN

GIANNA was so proud of herself that she sang while she cleaned the living-room—bits from stage musicals, old popular songs, a ballad here and there. When she found herself humming a lullaby from her childhood, though, she had to laugh. 'Aren't we becoming domestic?' she jeered. The last time she had heard that lullaby had been in the old house. She'd been nine or ten, perhaps. She'd been miserably ill that winter, and her mother had found her one day in a bout of frustrated tears. Carol had held her like a baby, and sung the lullaby of long ago to her . . .

So the new owners of their old house had terrible taste in wallpaper, Gianna thought as she pulled the couch away from the wall to clean behind it. Maybe she should go and look at the house, after all. Even if the tour accomplished nothing else, at least it would get the longing for home out of her mind, once and for all.

'But what if it just makes me want it more?' she asked herself. That was possible, too—that seeing the house again would actually increase her longing to get away from a cramped little apartment.

And if so, why shouldn't she have it? She was making good money at Westway, and the company was solid. She could afford to take on a mortgage if she wanted to.

But could she afford the time? she asked herself. There would be things like lawn mowing, and leaf raking, and snow shovelling—all the things that an apartment-dweller never had to be concerned with. If she bought the house, someone would have to take care of the garden, and the flowers. And she'd need a housekeeper of some sort. She could hardly keep up with a three-room apartment now; how could she realistically expect to manage a house? The house had more space on the ground floor than there was in herwhole apartment.

'Don't be ridiculous,' she lectured herself. 'You can't possibly keep up with the demands of a house in the suburbs!'

But it would eliminate the long commute to work. It would be like having an extra hour a day, if she didn't have to drive across Chicago every morning and evening. With an extra hour, she could do a lot of house-cleaning. And it would be so nice to have more space. There would be room for her collections, for her books. And more than that, there would be the sense of permanence that a house provided, the feeling of solidity, the visual evidence of what her work was accomplishing.

'It can't possibly hurt to look,' she told herself, sounding more certain than she felt. She reached for the telephone book. Elliot, wasn't that what her mother had said the agent's name was? There couldn't be to many Elliots in the Yellow Pages under real estate . . .

Mr Elliot's office was in a suburb near Oak Park. Gianna jotted the number down, and noticed that Mr Elliot even listed his home telephone number, for calls after regular business hours. 'That's thoughtful of him,' she mused.

She tucked the slip of paper into the side pocket of her handbag. She'd think about it, she decided, and perhaps tomorrow she'd call Mr Elliot. After all, she would only be looking. A person could look at a hundred houses without making any commitment to buy one.

And perhaps, she thought, looking around wouldn't be such a bad idea, either. Just because she had fond memories of that particular house it didn't mean that she had to have it to be happy. There were other houses, smaller ones that would be easier to manage, all over the suburbs. Perhaps there was a house somewhere that would be just right for her. Maybe it was just waiting for her to come along.

She pushed the couch back against the wall and started to move chairs. The apartment hadn't been this clean in ages, she told herself cheerfully, and she could take all the credit herself. She'd been the one who managed to fix the silly vacuum cleaner.

The telephone rang, and she shut the vacuum off and went to answer it. Probably it's Norman, she thought, calling to tell me that Cluny found out about him inviting me, and raised the roof.

'Hi,' said Blake.

'Are you home already?' She sounded just a little breathless from the physical work.

'No. I'm still at the plant. But it just occurred to me that you might be left high and dry tomorrow. Would you like me to call Curtis and see if we can make a foursome of it?'

The warm feeling that had swept over her with the first sound of his voice vanished. Go on a double date with Blake and Meghan—with Curtis as her companion? The very idea! Blake was treating her like some poor relation who couldn't possibly get a date without assistance!

'No, thanks,' she said sweetly. 'I've managed to find myself some entertainment for New Year's Eve, without your help.'

He didn't sound upset. He probably was delighted, Gianna fumed; with his conscience clear, he could really enjoy his evening with Meghan! 'That's good,' he said. 'I'm glad you won't be alone.'

'Don't worry about me. I'm quite able to look after myself.'

'Of course you are. No one has ever said you weren't.' His tone was polite. 'I'll be finished here in another half hour or so. Have you eaten, or are you still interested in Chinese?'

Gianna considered for a moment. The food sounded good; she'd become so involved in her cleaning that she'd forgotten about eating. But when she weighed that against the aggravation she was feeling towards Blake just now, she decided that she'd rather die of starvation than give him the impression that she couldn't do without him. Heaven forbid that he thinks she'd been sitting beside the phone waiting for him to call!

'I've eaten,' she lied evenly. 'Some other time, perhaps. Now, unless there's something really important, Blake, I was busy when you called.'

If she had hoped for him to be intrigued, or puzzled, or anxious to find out what was absorbing her, she was disappointed. Blake hesitated only an instant before saying coolly, 'See you tomorrow, then,' and the telephone clicked against her ear.

She sat there thoughtfully for a moment. Perhaps buying the house was an even better idea than she had thought. It might be a good idea to move into a place that was really her own, she decided. Living down the hall from Blake had seemed like a good idea at the time, but perhaps there was such a thing as too much togetherness. And especially now that he had found Meghan——

'Meghan has nothing to do with it,' Gianna told herself firmly. 'I'm a grown woman, and it's time for me to be completely independent. Blake means well, and all that, but as long as I'm living next door to him, I won't really be on my own.'

She glanced at her watch and decided it was too late to call Mr Elliot now. She'd try his office in the morning.

It was comforting to have made a decision, and she went back to her cleaning with a will.

I can make it on my own, she thought. I'm an intelligent, capable woman, and I can do anything I make up my mind to do. I don't need Blake for anything.

Then she turned on the vacuum cleaner again, and watched in horror as it belched clouds of dust—the very dust she had just patiently cleaned from carpets and furniture—back into the air.

Perhaps, she admitted, it wasn't going to be quite so easy to wipe Blake out of her life.

New Year's Eve—and it seemed that everyone in Chicago was celebrating. Cluny's party was a booming success; the party room was crowded with people in silly hats, with noisemakers, even though midnight was still an hour away. The buffet table was loaded with snacks, and the glasses were always full. Gianna sipped her champagne and shook her head at Norman when he tried to refill her glass.

'I'm on my second glass now,' she protested.

'Oh, come on. It's New Year—live a little!' He splashed the bubbly liquid into her glass. It overflowed the rim and splattered across her skirt.

Norman, she thought, had had plenty of champagne already himself. His cheeks were flushed, his eyes bright, and his timid air had almost vanished. On the whole, Gianna thought, she preferred him when he was being shy.

Gianna knew most of the people whom Cluny had invited, and she should have been enjoying the party. But she felt as if she was at a distance from it all, observing through a window that let bursts of noise come through, but did not permit her to touch the people or feel the warmth. Worse than that, she thought, she didn't really care. She didn't want to come out of the corner and try to be the life of the party.

She sighed. She knew what was causing her dissatisfaction tonight; there was no sense in ignoring it. When she and Norman had come in, it had been impossible to miss the sensation in the outer restaurant—the sensation caused by one famous model and her adoring escort being mobbed by fans. There had even, unless Gianna missed her guess, been a couple of reporters in that throng.

Yes, it had been impossible for her to miss the excitement. She didn't think Blake had seen her, however; she doubted, in fact, if he had even noticed the mob, because he was so absorbed in Meghan. He'd been staring down into those lovely green eyes, and he had just raised Meghan's long, slim hand to his lips when Gianna had walked past. Frankly, she thought, he probably wouldn't have noticed a torpedo striking the next table, much less one young woman walking by with her date . . .

What was the matter with the man? she raged to herself. Couldn't he see beyond Meghan's beauty?

She sighed. In any case, she was forced to admit that what Blake did was his choice, and nothing to do with her. She put him firmly out of her mind, and thought about herself instead.

It had been an eventful year, she thought idly. A new and empty one stretched out before her. What would it bring? The new perfume—would it be smash hit, or flop, or something unexpectedly in-between? She had an uneasy feeling about it, as if she had unknowingly let a monster loose in the corporate offices.

And the monster's name, Gianna told herself, is Meghan. She tried to stifle the thought; it was none of her business how Blake conducted his life, after all. Even if he decided that he wanted to marry Meghan—and it seemed likely, considering that he had even thought of bringing her home for Christmas, that he was thinking of doing so—it couldn't possibly make any difference to Gianna. But she was uncomfortable about it, anyway. For one thing, she didn't believe that Meghan could be serious about Blake. And, if Meghan dumped Blake, he might blame Gianna for the hurt, simply because it had been her idea to bring Meghan into the project in the first place.

As if it would be my fault, she thought. I'm not the one who's responsible! He got himself into this. I certainly didn't ask her to date him.

And yet, uneasily, she wasn't quite sure that concern for Blake's feelings was all that was bothering her. What if Meghan didn't reject him? What if she was tired of the modelling game, and decided that Blake was a good catch?

By the end of the new year, Gianna thought, everything might have changed. This might be the last time that things were calm, and settled, and peaceful. It made her feel a little sad, and a little scared.

She told herself she was being silly. There was nothing magical about the ending of a year, after all—it was only a means of counting time. There was nothing different about this night from any other in the calendar. And tomorrow would be just another day.

Norman came up behind her and dropped a kiss on the nape of her neck. Gianna shied away from him.

'What's the matter?' he asked.

'You startled me.'

He laughed a little. 'Surely you know how crazy I am about you,' he said. His voice was a little unsteady.

'No,' she said. 'To tell the truth, I didn't know anything of the sort.'

'Well, I am. And it's almost midnight, and I want to be kissing you when the clock strikes.'

And what about me? Gianna thought. What if I don't want to be kissing you?

Be a sport, she told herself. It's New Year's Eve, and you won't ever have to spend another evening in the company of this man. Everybody will be kissing everybody in another few minutes; it doesn't mean a thing.

The countdown of the final seconds to midnight had started. 'Ten—nine——' The chorus grew as more guests joined in.

Last New Year's Eve, Gianna thought, Blake and I were drinking champagne and playing gin rummy in his living-room. And when the clock struck, he kissed me on the cheek and said 'Gin,' and won the game ...

That's quite an unusual event to be sentimental over, she jeered at herself. What a memory to tuck away to tell her grandchildren about! They would probably laugh her out of the room. And Blake's grandchildren—well, they would want to hear all about the New Year's Eve he'd spent with the famous Meghan.

But maybe, Gianna thought, they wouldn't put it that way at all. Maybe they'd be asking him instead about the first New Year's Eve he'd spent with their famous grandmother——

Oh, stop it! she told herself crossly. What did Cluny put in this champagne, anyway? It must be something; I haven't been so depressed in a long time.

'Five—four——'

Norman's arms closed around her, and his mouth came down firmly on hers. The fumes of alcohol were enough to make her dizzy.

'Three—two—one——Happy New Year!' The voices rang in chorus. Noisemakers shrilled. Someone tossed handfuls of confetti.

The kiss seemed to last for ever, but Gianna was sure it could only have been a matter of seconds before a hand landed on Norman's shoulder. 'Come on, Norm,' a voice urged. 'Break it up and join the party!'

She sighed in relief and stepped away from him, and from then on made it a point to keep at least two people between them. More champagne was brought out, and more trays of snacks. The noisemakers were shrilling incessantly. Gianna brushed confetti out of her hair with her fingers, and watched the flakes of multicoloured paper mingle with the layer already on the floor. The restaurant management was going to be very unhappy about this, she thought. She was glad it was Cluny who would have to explain it.

The party would probably go on till dawn, or until the law required the restaurant to close, but Gianna wasn't going to stay around for more. She had forgotten just how boring a party could be, when everyone else was drinking too much.

Amateur night, Blake called New Year's Eve, because even people who seldom partied at all used it as an excuse to go out, celebrate, and make fools of themselves. That was why she and Blake usually stayed at home, cooked a gourmet meal, talked or played a game——

Her head was hurting from the noise. New Year's Eve parties really were a bore, she thought. She realised that

Norman was standing beside her, a fresh glass of champagne in his hand, and she said, 'I'm very tired, Norman. I'm going home. Thanks for inviting me.'

'I'm going to take you home,' he told her.

Gianna shrugged. What difference did it make? She had expected him to resist leaving the party, but if he wanted to take her home, she wouldn't object. She wasn't fond of the idea of hailing a cab and getting herself home at this hour of New Year's Day.

Once outside in the cold night air, though, she began to have second thoughts. The first blast of wind nearly knocked Norman off his feet. Just how much has he had to drink? she wondered uneasily, but before she could talk him into letting her go alone, she was in a cab.

The taxi was warm, and long before they reached Gianna's apartment, Norman was sweating profusely and shedding gloves, hat, and scarf. He would have taken his coat off if Gianna hadn't stopped him.

He reeled out of the cab as soon as it stopped, and held the door for her. Gianna told the cabby, 'I think you'd better take the gentleman home.'

'No!' Norman protested, 'I want a cup of coffee.'

'I'm not crazy enough to haul him any further, lady,' the cabby said. 'Whenever I can get rid of a drunk, I do it.'

'But——' Her protest was ignored.

Norman paid the cabby with a grand gesture, slammed the door, and held out an unsteady arm to Gianna.

'Well, perhaps one cup of coffee,' she said reluctantly. There was no point in making a scene on the sidewalk.

The doorman took one look at Norman, and turned a quizzical eye on Gianna.

'Mr Brown is coming up for one cup of coffee,' she said. 'He'll be leaving in fifteen minutes or so.' The doorman nodded, and Gianna breathed a little easier. If Norman hadn't appeared in the lobby inside of a quarter of an hour, the doorman would call her apartment to find out what the problem was. It was a code they had worked out long ago, and Gianna had never been more thankful for a nosy doorman on duty.

Norman tried to kiss her in the elevator. When she said, firmly 'Some other time, Norman,' he started to pout. It gave her second thoughts about giving him even one cup of coffee. It would take much more than one cup to sober Norman. Besides, if she let him in at all, how was she to get rid of him? The doorman wasn't exactly a bouncer. Even if he could leave his post and come up to her floor—which he really wasn't supposed to do—he'd have a tough time evicting Norman if Norman didn't want to be evicted.

At the door of her apartment, she paused. 'Thanks for a good time, Norman,' she said.

'You said I could come in for coffee.' He sounded like an obstinate child.

'But it's late, and——'

'You said I could come in for coffee!' His voice was getting louder.

'Norman, how about if we have coffee some other——'

'You said——' This time the words almost echoed off the walls.

Obviously that approach wasn't working well. In a minute or two, disapproving heads would be starting to poke out of doors up and down the halls.

'Norman, if you come in for one cup, then will you go home without an argument?' said Gianna firmly.

He nodded.

I should have left him in the lobby, Gianna thought. Why didn't I realise what shape he was in?

Because he didn't really have all that much to drink, she told herself. Obviously he wasn't used to partying like that. It took a harder head than Norman's to keep up with Cluny's friends.

She unlocked the door and led him into the living

room. 'You just sit down here,' she said, 'and I'll go fix the coffee.'

He looked for a moment as if he was going to rebel, but he obeyed. Gianna sighed in relief and went to the kitchen.

Now what am I supposed to do with him? she wondered. Well, the first thing was the promised coffee. She started the pot brewing and then leaned against the kitchen counter, waiting. She didn't want to go back into that room with him just now.

She wetted the corner of a dishtowel and scrubbed at the champagne stains on her skirt. Darn Norman, anyway, she thought. The stains probably wouldn't come out, and the dress was brand new. She sighed and put the towel down. Maybe the dry-cleaners could remove the mess.

Ten minutes later, when she carried the tray into the living room, Norman was stretched out on the couch, snoring. Gianna swore under her breath and set the tray down on the low table, and just then the telephone rang. The doorman, she thought, was right on schedule.

'Miss West?' he asked anxiously. 'Are you all right?'

'I'm fine. Mr Brown will be on his way in a few minutes.'

There was a second's hesitation. 'I'm sorry if I bothered you,' he said. 'But I thought perhaps the gentleman might give you some trouble.'

'Thank you for calling to check on me, but I can handle it this time.' I'll just wake him up, pour his coffee into him, and send him on his way, she thought. Nothing to it.

'Very good, Miss West.'

She put the phone down and bent over the sleeping form on the couch. 'Norman,' she said.

He murmured something unintelligible. She shook him, a little, and called his name again.

His eyes opened, and he smiled cherubically up at her. His hands closed on her wrists, and he pulled.

Off balance, Gianna struggled to keep herself from

falling. She caught at the back of the couch. 'Norman!' she protested.

He tugged again, and she landed awkwardly on top of him on the couch.

'Don't you want your coffee?' she asked.

His voice was muffled against her throat. 'There are things I want a whole lot more than coffee,' he said. 'And I think you do, too, Gianna.'

Panic began to nibble at the corners of her mind, and she struggled. He held her easily, and sprawled as she was, she couldn't get enough of a hold to push away from him. 'Dammit, Norman, let me go!' she cried.

Instead, he pulled her down closer. His breath was hot against her face, and the fumes from the champagne seemed to blister her skin. What do I do now? she wondered, and cursed silently at the doorman. Why couldn't he have called just two minutes later?

It isn't his fault, she reminded herself. You're the idiot who assured him that everything was all right.

She thought she heard the familiar click of a key in the door. Or was she only dreaming it? After all, the doorman certainly wouldn't have come up. And who else could be at her door? A burglar, she thought wildly. It would be just my luck tonight . . .

'Just what's going on in here?' Blake asked coolly.

Gianna twisted around on the couch and stared at him. What was he doing here? He was with Meghan, celebrating the night away! 'Blake!' she whispered.

He came slowly across the room. She thought she had never seen quite that menacing look on his face before. But all he said was 'I'm sure you won't mind explaining this, Norman.'

Norman pushed Gianna away and sat up hastily. 'She invited me up,' he began.

The little coward! thought Gianna.

Norman ran his fingers through his hair and darted a look at her as he said, 'I—I didn't realise I was trespassing on your territory, Blake.'

'Well, you are,' Blake said coldly.

'But you were Cluny's date that night——'

'Goodbye, Norman.'

'And you were with that model tonight——'

Blake took hold of a handful of Norman's shoulder and hauled him off the couch. 'I said goodnight, Norman.'

'Yes, sir,' Norman mumbled. It was almost a babble. He grabbed his coat. 'I'll see you later, Gianna.'

'Over my dead body,' muttered Blake.

Norman's eyes widened. 'I meant, I'll see you around, probably. Nothing more. I'll——' He looked down at his coat. 'I'll put this on in the elevator,' he decided, and fled to the door.

The instant it closed behind him, Blake burst into laughter.

Gianna didn't see the humour. 'What do you mean, over your dead body?' she demanded.

'You have such terrific taste in men, Gianna,' grinned Blake.

She was furious. 'You implied that I—that you——'

'That we're living together? Yes, I did. Would you rather I'd have tried to explain it to him? I'm afraid it might have come to a fight, if I'd told him I was merely a friend.'

'I don't even know why you're here!'

'Easily explained.' Blake was standing in the centre of the room, perfectly at ease, his hands in his pockets. He was casually dressed. He'd been home then for a while, she thought. 'The doorman wasn't quite convinced that Norman was harmless, even after you assured him that all was well. So he called me and suggested I check on you.'

'Well, isn't that just jolly of him?' Gianna was furious, especially because he was right. 'Well, it's none of his business—or yours, either—who I bring up here!'

Blake raised an eyebrow. 'Oh? I thought I heard you say, "Dammit, Norman, let me go!" Is this just a new style in making love? Perhaps I'm further behind the times than I thought.'

She licked her dry lips. What was wrong with her? she wondered. She should be throwing herself on him with tears of gratitude right about now. Instead, she was so embarrassed at the idea of the scene he had walked in on that she could just start to scream.

'I didn't need your help,' she said stiffly.

'Oh, you enjoy being manhandled?' He took his hands out of his pockets. 'In that case, I'm sorry I interfered in your pleasure. I suppose the least I can do is replace your friend Norman—as far as my limited talents allow.'

Gianna backed away from him. 'Blake, you're drunk!'

'No. But I'll do my best to pretend, if that's what you found so attractive about Norman.'

She was having trouble breathing. 'Blake, don't be an idiot——'

'Are you sure you're sober yourself? You smell like you fell into a wine vat.'

'Norman spilled champagne on me at the party.' His arms were around her, and she struggled. It was like trying to fight her way out of a steel net.

'And you still brought him home? I can see I'll have to pretend harder than I thought.'

'Blake, don't——'

'You can call me Norman if you'd rather.' His arms cradled her, lowering her gently to the floor. 'It might help with the atmosphere, and let me really get into the character.

'Listen, just because Meghan wanted to go home early, you don't have to take it out on me!'

He ignored her. He was holding her down on the carpet by then, his body hard and relentless against her. She fought to get a hand free, and he captured both her wrists, tugged her arms above her head, and pinned them there with one hand. His other hand caressed her temple, her cheek, her throat, before settling like a warm blanket across her breast.

She struggled against him, but his weight made it impossible for her to free herself. 'What are you trying to prove?' she gasped.

'That you can't protect yourself from a drunken bum like Norman,' he said. His mouth was hot against her throat.

Gianna tossed her head wildly. 'I wasn't afraid of Norman,' she whispered, with a catch in her voice.

That stopped him. He lay very still for a long moment. 'And you are afraid of me?'

She nodded miserably. She was too terrified to fight him any more.

'Oh, Gianna,' he whispered. 'I didn't mean for you to be afraid of me——' He released her arms slowly. She flexed the muscles a little, almost afraid to move.

He turned his head, and she stared up into his hazel eyes. She saw his intention there, even before he bent his head to kiss her, and she closed her eyes. Perhaps if she couldn't see him, she thought, she could pretend it wasn't happening.

It was not so easy. If the kisses they had shared beside the fireplace on Christmas Eve had been like fire-crackers going off inside her, this was like a ton of dynamite. Every square inch of her skin shivered away from him, and at the same instant craved his touch. Every fibre of her body wanted him to leave her alone, and also frantically hoped that he would show her what making love was really all about . . . Her body slackened, softened, welcomed his caresses.

'Gianna?' His voice was hoarse.

She was heartily ashamed of herself. She put a hand across her eyes, trying to shut out the sight of him and the knowledge of what she had almost asked of him. 'Go away, Blake,' she begged. It was a raspy whisper.

For a long moment he lay there, and when he pulled himself away she almost cried out, begging him to come back to her, not to leave her there alone. But she stifled the words, and didn't look at him, though she knew he stood beside her for a long moment.

Then, without a word, he was gone. Gianna lay there on the cold carpet for a long time.

I wanted him to make love to me, she thought. He's always been my best friend, but suddenly that's not enough any more. I want more than his friendship now. That's why I've been so angry with him over Meghan. It's happened so slowly that I didn't even know I wanted him for myself.

Just when, she wondered, had her fondness for Blake—the fondness of a girl for a favourite brother—changed? When had it become, instead, the love of a woman for a man?

CHAPTER EIGHT

SHE knew it, now. Knew it with every cell, every delicate nerve. She had loved him always, as a friend and as a brother. Now . . . 'I want to love him as my husband,' she said painfully.

Hearing the words didn't make it any easier. She dragged herself up from the carpet and straightened her skirt, kicked off her shoes, pulled out the combs that had held her hair up in the sophisticated style. Not so sophisticated now, she thought, after she'd been mauled by two different men.

Such very different men. Norman's touch had horrified her; the sudden change from shy boy to demanding man had frightened her. Not that she had been any less frightened with Blake, she admitted, but it had been a very different sort of fear—the fear that she would lose control. The fear that she might end up in bed with him, of her own free will.

And if she had, she thought defiantly, what would it have mattered? They were adults.

No, she realised, the fear of sleeping with him hadn't been the problem at all. It was a different fear that had tormented her—the fear that Blake would have been the one to reject her, had they shared one more mad moment on the carpet. As it was, he had been the one who pulled away—reminded, perhaps, of Meghan.

Meghan, she thought. Had the model gone home for a good night's sleep, afraid to risk her beauty for a late night? Or had she, perhaps, been waiting for him in his apartment—maybe even in his bed?

Not a chance, Gianna told herself. If Meghan had

been waiting for him, he wouldn't have been on the floor with me!

Or would he? He hadn't intended the episode to go as far as it had, she was sure of that. He had meant merely to give her a lesson in how quickly things could get out of hand.

Some lesson, she thought drearily. He'd proved that much, all right. And as soon as he had realised it, he had been gone. Which was all the answer she needed; the episode had frightened him so much that he had fled.

She stared out the window at the golden lights of Chicago, a glistening blanket beneath her window. The streets were black ribbons where the snow had been scraped away, and light traffic was moving smoothly along Lake Shore Drive. The city's pace slowed in the middle of the night, but it never came to a halt.

But Gianna wasn't thinking about the jewelled landscape beneath her window. Her thoughts were just as chaotic as the random traffic patterns.

You got yourself into this, she accused. You're the one who brought Meghan into the picture. You're the one who got jealous, and threw a wrench into the closeness you need to have with Blake.

Meghan might be the serpent in the garden of Eden, she reflected, but it was Gianna herself who had invited her in.

'Everything was jolly until you created this disaster,' she told herself. 'You set yourself up, Gianna. Now, what are you going to do about it?'

There was no answer. Finally, exhausted, she crept into her bed. Eventually, fitfully, she slept, and dreamed of a giant red apple that harboured a worm—a worm who wore Meghan's lovely face.

Mr Elliot was reluctant to show Gianna the house. 'I'm almost certain it's sold,' he told her. 'The people who looked at it last week are going to make an offer, as soon as they have a chance to discuss it with their banker. And I hate to show it again until I know for sure.'

Gianna couldn't believe what she was hearing. A real-estate person who didn't want to show a house? She almost said, but you showed it to my mother, and there's no one less interested in buying a house than she is!

'It's such an inconvenience for them, you see,' he explained. 'The owners, I mean. They have small children, and they'd simply rather not have droves of people coming through——'

'One person is scarcely a drove,' Gianna pointed out. 'And I certainly don't expect it to look like a showcase. I'm looking at the rooms; I can ignore the toys and clutter.'

He looked down his nose at her. 'It would be such a shame if you were to fall in love with that house, and then find there's no chance of buying it. It's been known to happen before, and it's very disappointing for the clients. I have several other houses you might be interested in, Miss West——'

'I want to see that one,' Gianna said. 'Show me that one first, and then we'll talk about others.'

'But I really think——'

'If you're concerned about whether I could afford it, don't worry,' she said pointedly. 'But if you don't want to show it, I'm sure another agent will. It's included in the multiple listings, I assume?'

He sighed. 'Very well, Miss West. I think it's a waste of your time, however, because I'm certain it's already all but sold.'

'It's very kind of you to be concerned about my time,' Gianna told him gently.

He didn't have an answer to that one, but she could tell from the quality of the silence that he was annoyed.

'Perhaps you'll end up with a bidding war on your hands,' she went on sweetly. 'If I like the house, that is.' She hadn't told him that she had grown up there; he hadn't allowed her to get that far.

He rang the following morning and said she could look at the house if she could be there within half an hour. She was certain he'd done it on purpose, waiting till the last minute in the hope that she would back out. Instead, she told him she'd be right there, and she had shoved aside the latest research and development reports. She hadn't been learning much from them anyway; it was hard to stay interested in a prospective new skin-conditioning cream when her mind kept skipping off to other things. It would be nice to have a little cold, fresh air—perhaps it would blow some of the cobwebs out of her brain and let her concentrate.

'If Mr Whittaker comes back, tell him I've been called away for an hour,' she instructed the secretary.

'Of course, Miss West.' The secretary's voice was level, but her tone was sympthetic. She knew there was trouble, that was apparent from the way she looked at Gianna these days. Giana fervently hoped the secretary hadn't figured out what had caused the problem.

She had scarcely seen Blake in the last few days. He had been out all New Year's Day. With Meghan, she supposed, with a twinge of sadness. The day after that, the ad agency had started to work on the photo sessions with Meghan, and since then Blake had spent most of his time in the studio, watching each set-up. Even when he was in the plant, he closeted himself in his office with the paperwork. Gianna had barely caught a glimpse of him in days.

He's as embarrassed as I am, she thought as she drove across Oak Park to the old house. And he doesn't want to take any chances of it happening again. 'As if I'd let it!' she said aloud.

Then she made a face at herself. 'You're a liar, Gianna West,' she told herself glumly.

He can't stand to look at me, she thought sadly, because of the memories it dredges up. I hope the house works out so I can move. It would be much better for both of us if we didn't have to be afraid of running into each other around the clock.

There was a little sadness, though, at the idea of leaving the apartment. It had been her home for only a few months, but those months had been happy ones. Sunday mornings, when they shared coffee and dough-nuts and the newspaper in companionable silence, usually with both of them still half asleep. Evenings in Orchestra Hall, just a few blocks away, with the power of the Chicago Symphony swelling around them, filling the huge auditorium to the ornate ceiling. The memories crowded in on her—watching the ballet performance of *The Nutcracker*, every Christmas season. Bicycling in Grant Park in the soft springtime. Boating on Lake Michigan. All with Blake beside her, laughing and teasing——

'Let's not be maudlin,' she told herself firmly. 'If you don't stop this, you'll be crying in a moment!'

There was little activity on the quiet streets, still slippery in patches from the packed snow and ice of the last storm. When she reached the old neighbourhood, there was no evidence of Mr Elliot. Gianna parked her car on the street in front of the big white house. There was plenty of room for it around the back, she knew, but she didn't feel quite right about driving in as if she owned the place. Not yet, at any rate.

She propped an elbow against the car door and studied the house. Funny, she thought, but she had never noticed before that it was such an odd mixture of styles of architecture. Nondescript, she decided; that was the best word for it. With a dormer style borrowed from the Victorians, and a porch that was modified from the Colonials, all tacked on to a basic, solid cube, it was unlike any other house she'd ever seen. Yes, it was nondescript, but it was also comfortable, she thought. Not an architectural showpiece by any stretch of the imagination, but a good place to raise a family ...

And whatever had brought that thought to mind? she wondered irritably.

The house was plain white, with black shutters. The wide, welcoming front porch was supported by clusters of pillars. The roof line included the most unusual feature, a double-peaked dormer that added interest to the whole house. The lawn was broad and well kept, stretching out to the street under the shade of two huge old maple trees. She had always wanted to build a tree house in one of them, but her father would never let her.

It hadn't been fair, she thought. Blake had a tree house. That was probably the only reason she had wanted one, she decided with a tender smile. She simply had not wanted to be outdone.

A station wagon pulled up behind her car and a short, bald man got out. The reluctant Mr Elliot, she assumed, and stepped out of her car. 'Good afternoon,' she said pleasantly.

'Miss West?' Mr Elliot looked a little surprised. He was pulling out a key. 'We'll have to hurry,' he said.

I've never seen anyone so devoted to his job, Gianna thought with a touch of irony. Or does he think no woman my age could possibly afford a house in this neighbourhood?

She had wondered if walking into the front hall would be like stepping back in time, and for the first instant it was almost like seeing a ghost. The hall as it was seemed to be superimposed on her memories of how it used to be. it was almost like seeing double.

But the odd reaction lasted only an instant. Then it was like any other hallway, with a mahogany staircase curving up to the circular landing above. That was the only thing that remained of the room she had known. Even the carpeting was new, a plush earth tone that was as soft as an eiderdown under foot.

She turned automatically to the right, to the long

living-room. It and the small den that lay beyond it were just as she remembered them, apart from the new carpet. The fireplace in the centre of the long wall was where they had always gathered in the evenings. The den, lined with low bookshelves and huge windows, was where she had thrown herself into a deep chair to escape into a book and daydream of bright tomorrows. The den was three steps higher than the living-room, and it was on this carved staircase, when she was three years old, that Gianna had learned to slide down a banister. Blake had taught her, and Carol had been furious with him, Gianna remembered vaguely. She smiled a little, caressing the satiny wood with the palm of her hand.

Mr Elliot sighed, as if impatient at how long she was taking. 'Across the hall is the dining-room, breakfast nook, and kitchen,' he told her. 'Also a back entry and a half-bath. Upstairs——'

'Three bedrooms, one sitting-room, and three baths,' Gianna murmured. 'On the third floor is another bedroom and bath. It was probably the maid's quarters originally.' She smiled at him genially and went back across the hall, ignoring his open-mouthed astonishment.

The first thing she saw in the dining-room was what her mother had called Art Deco wallpaper. It wasn't, strictly speaking, from that period, Gianna realised, but the huge motifs of butterflies and the geometric patterns of the edging certainly qualified it for the name. The shiny foil reflected the light from the chandelier, fracturing it into rainbows.

That's got to go, she thought, and realised she was thinking as if she already owned the house.

Let's not be ridiculous, she told herself. I haven't even seen the whole thing yet.

'What's the asking price?' she enquired, turning her back on the distracting wallpaper.

Mr Elliot consulted a pocket notebook and told her. Gianna swallowed hard. It was almost twice what her parents had sold the house for. She walked through the rest of the house in silence. The third floor, which had been her teenage haven, was now a playroom for the children. The kitchen had been painted mustard yellow, instead of Carol's soft peach. But there was nothing wrong that couldn't be easily fixed. And the idea of owning her own bit of land, her own house, was an attractive one.

'I may want to make a bid on the house,' she said, as they retraced their steps to the cars.

For the first time, Mr Elliot sounded mildly interested. 'Oh? What sort of offer do you have in mind?'

'At the moment, I don't know. But I think they've set the price too high.'

'That's where you're wrong, Miss West. This house isn't going to be on the market long.'

'I don't know how you expect to sell it in a hurry when you don't even want to show it,' Gianna said drily.

'I'm not violating confidence if I tell you that the bid these other people will be making is very nearly the asking price,' Mr Elliot told her.

Gianna wondered if that was a standard ploy, and if, in fact, the 'other people' were only a myth intended to increase the amount she was willing to pay for the house. But she smiled sweetly, got in her car, and said, 'In that case, they may have it with my blessing.'

He made a sound something like a snort. 'If the bid falls through, or the owners don't accept it, I'll certainly be in touch, Miss West. But, if you take my advice, you'll let me show you some other houses.'

She smiled. 'Let's see what happens to this one first, shall we?'

She spent the evening thinking about the house. So much for the idea that by looking at the house she could get this foolish idea out of her head! Seeing the house again, even changed as it was, had brought back long-buried memories of home. The heavy, yeasty smell of bread baking as she came in from school. The satiny texture of the couch in the den against her cheek as she lay there to read. The rhythmic pounding from the basement workshop, where her father always had a project underway.

She stared at the ceiling of her apartment, with its glittery texture applied in a matter of minutes with a special sprayer when the building was built, and thought about the geometric shapes painstakingly carved and cast in plaster in the ceilings of the house. She was fairly sure she could have it, if she was willing to pay the price. After all, Mr Elliot's other clients hadn't even made a formal offer. But the question was, just how badly did she want it?

She sighed, got her wallet out of her handbag, put on her coat, and went out into the cold. She had forgotten to stop to buy food on her way home, and there was nothing in the apartment that she wanted to eat. Winter was no time to let supplies run low, she reminded herself. A storm could hit at any moment.

What she was really longing for, she admitted as she pushed a trolley through the supermarket, was not the house itself, but all the things it represented. The closeness of family life, the permanence and security of ownership. Those were the things she was searching for, not that particular house at all.

She picked up a sandwich and a salad at the delicatessen, and stood in the checkout lane looking at the small pile of goods in the cart. She had bought convenience foods, mostly. Some of them she didn't even remember picking up; she had selected them out of habit.

Let's be honest, Gianna, she told herself. You wouldn't cook, no matter what sort of kitchen you had. You're not like your mother, and there's no sense in pretending you are.

She hadn't suffered from this longing for home before,

she realised. It had only been after she had felt Blake pulling away that she had begun to dream of home. Most of those things she was wishing for had been hers, before that. She had Blake's companionship, then. She had the security and solidity of their friendship. She hadn't been aware of anything that might be lacking.

And then Gwen had to go and tell Blake that she thought he should marry Gianna, and everything had gone down the drain. That was when things had started to change, she thought, even before Meghan had come on the scene. It was all Gwen's fault——

Hold it! she thought. Don't blame everything on Gwen. You were the one who was too idiotic to know that his friendship wasn't going to be enough to satisfy you.

And what difference would it have made if she had known that she loved him? she asked herself angrily. What could she have done—announce it? That would only have driven him away faster!

The line was long and slow. Everyone, it seemed, had chosen this evening to stock up on staples. Gianna turned her attention to the tabloid newspapers displayed beside the checkout lines.

'Abominable Snowman Terrifies Two in Wisconsin,' one headline screamed. Across another front page a photograph was splashed, showing an elderly woman cradling an infant—her fifty-third child and a new world's record, the caption proclaimed. A third paper, half hidden behind the snowman one, screeched, 'Meghan's Mystery——' The rest of the headline was concealed.

'Who cares?' muttered Gianna. 'They've probably uncovered the banana split scandal.' But she reached for the paper anyway, hating herself for doing so.

It wasn't a good picture of Meghan; it was grainy and just a little fuzzy. But there was no mistaking where it had been taken, or when. The full headline read,

'Meghan's Mystery Man,' and the man beside the model was Blake. Their cosy New Year's Eve celebration was now no secret to the world.

Gianna dropped the newspaper back into its slot as quickly as if it had been obscene. She supposed she should have expected it; Meghan was hot news, and the tabloids would not miss an opportunity to build their readership by featuring her. She wondered if Blake knew about this.

'I'll help you now,' the checkout girl said in a long-suffering tone, and Gianna looked up, startled, to see that the customers ahead of her had vanished and that she was now holding up the line.

'Sorry,' she muttered, and pushed her trolley forward to start unloading her purchases. The line of items glided down the conveyor belt, and Gianna reached into the newspaper rack again. She would put Blake's picture in her scrapbook, she thought. Or hang it on her bathroom mirror, to remind herself each day of how foolish it would be to think that ordinary Gianna West might be able to take him away from the glamorous Meghan.

The doorman smiled at her as she came through the lobby with her bag of groceries. Did he know, she wondered, what had happened up in her apartment that night? Had Norman said anything to him, as he staggered out of the building? Or had Blake——

Her cheeks burned at the thought of having to be rescued by Blake, and at the memory of the aftermath. She set her bag down in the elevator and leaned against the wall, her eyes closed, off guard for a moment. In an instant, in her imagination, she was back in Blake's arms again. She could smell the sharp tang of his cologne, and she could feel the heat of his body against hers. Surely, surely she hadn't imagined that he, too, had felt the magic between them——

She opened her eyes and met Meghan's stare from the front page of the tabloid, arranged carefully on top of the bag of groceries so that it didn't get crumpled.

'If I was anything special to him,' Gianna told herself coldly, trying to drown any hope that she still nurtured in the secret corners of her heart, 'he would have said something long ago. Blake is no child. He knows what he wants, and who he wants. And he's made it apparent that he wants me to be his friend . . .'

Friend! For a moment she contemplated picking up the plastic container of eggs and dashing them against the elevator door. Instead, she controlled her temper and walked down the hall to her own apartment.

She set the bag down and reached into the pocket of her jeans for her door keys. Her fingers met only emptiness.

'Oh, come on!' she muttered impatiently, and turned the pocket inside out. The pockets of her heavy fleece coat yielded only her car keys and her wallet. She closed her eyes and thought for a moment. Had she locked the deadbolt when she left? If so, she must have had the key. Or had she simply pulled the door shut behind her, and relied on the small lock built into the knob?

She rattled the door, and was almost sure the deadbolt wasn't locked. She had left her handbag sitting on the kitchen table, she was sure of that. In her hurry to escape from the apartment, she must have left her keys in the handbag.

'Dumb,' she told herself. 'Very, very dumb.'

She glared at the bag of groceries. She'd bought ice cream and frozen pizza; she hated to leave it sitting in the hallway while she trailed clear back down to the lobby to ask the doorman to come let her in. But the only alternative was to bang on Blake's door and ask him for the spare set of keys.

Always assuming he was home at all, she concluded. He might be anywhere tonight, for all she knew. She wasn't even sure he was sleeping at the apartment these days; he might be spending all his time with Meghan.

She decided to go downstairs, and she was half-way to the elevator before she straightened her spine and marched back to Blake's door. Dammit, she thought, I've got nothing to be ashamed of. There's no reason why I shouldn't ask him to let me into my apartment! That's why I gave him the spare key, after all.

She banged on the door, then listened. There was no soft murmur of music, no kitchen noise, nothing to show that the apartment was occupied at all. She hammered on it again, just in case. She would have gone in after the keys, even if Blake wasn't at home, without a thought— except that her key to his apartment was also in her handbag. 'Not the most brilliant thing you've ever done,' she muttered.

She had almost given up when the lock clicked and a sleepy-looking Blake peered out. 'I should have known,' he said blearily.

It made her angry. 'Believe me,' she said tartly, 'I wouldn't have bothered you if it hadn't been an emergency.'

His mouth seemed to tighten just a little, but his voice was level as he unhooked the chain and let her in. 'With you, one never knows which emergency to expect next,' he observed. 'Tell me, are you out of apples? Do you want to borrow my shampoo? Or are you perishing for a quick game of gin rummy?'

Gianna was irritated. 'I locked myself out of my apartment,' she told him.

'Oh. Nothing more original than that?' He tightened the belt of his terry robe. 'Why don't you find a hiding place for a spare key?'

'Dammit, Blake, I didn't lock myself out on purpose!' she snapped.

He opened a drawer in the coffee table and got out a key ring. 'I didn't say you had.'

'Well, you acted as if you thought I'd planned it.' She flung the words out as a challenge.

'It's just that it may not always be convenient for me to be disturbed.' He sounded cold, distant.

It stung Gianna's pride, and made her soul hurt a little. Was he really saying he didn't even want to be her friend any more?

'Are you planning some illicit activities?' she enquired acidly. 'Expecting to have Meghan up here, or something? Let me know when she's coming, and I'll try to hold the noise down next door so I don't disturb you.'

Blake smiled suddenly. 'Are you absolutely certain she isnt here right now?' he asked. His tone was pleasant, but it had an icy edge.

Gianna felt as if someone had hit her in the stomach with a boulder. You idiot! she told herself. It wasn't even midnight yet, and that was early for Blake to be in bed. Yet here he was, in his robe, his hair obviously fresh from the pillow——

She snatched the keys from his hand. 'I won't trouble you any further, Blake.'

'Just what do you have against Meghan?' Blake asked softly.

Gianna shifted from one foot to the other. What answer could she give to that? she wondered. 'Nothing,' she said stiffly.

'She thinks you're pretty special,' Blake went on.

She snorted.

'I'm quite serious, Gianna. She's told me several times how much she admires your many accomplishments.'

Gianna didn't answer. She stormed out of the door and down the hall, and once inside her own apartment she leaned against the kitchen counter for a moment, getting her breath back.

Oh, Meghan was a devil, she thought. So she had told Blake she was envious of Gianna, had she? It took a brilliant woman to figure out that defence. If she had attacked Gianna, she might have aroused Blake's protective instincts. Intead, she pretended to admire her, and lulled him into security. And what could Gianna say to him that would combat Meghan's influence? Nothing—for whatever she said would be written off as the ravings of a jealous woman.

Giana doubled up her fist and hit the counter as hard as she could. The pain shooting through her hand and wrist brought her back to reality.

'You're a jealous woman,' she told herself wearily. 'A very jealous woman.'

And with competition like Meghan, what hope was there that she could ever be anything more?

CHAPTER NINE

SHE couldn't beat Meghan if it came to a battle with Blake as the prize, that was for sure. Against that lovely face, the elegant body, the deferential manner, any other woman was bound to be a loser. Meghan was cool, graceful, poised.

And she's absolutely never a klutz like me, Gianna thought wearily. She probably never loses track of her keys.

She tossed against her pillow, got up and untangled the sheets, slid back between them and tossed some more. There was no sense in even thinking about persuading Blake to give Meghan up, she told herself. It couldn't be done, and the only thing she could accomplish by trying was to drive him away completely. Their friendship was already damaged; if she continued to quarrel with him over Meghan, it would soon reach the point where their business would also suffer.

Their partnership had been an unusual one from the beginning, with the responsibilities so evenly divided between them. It had always worked because of their respect for each other and their ability to function as a team. In some ways, they could almost read each other's minds, as the staff half believed. And even in the midst of their squabbles, they had both kept hold of their appreciation of the ridiculous. But Gianna didn't think Blake's sense of humour would function very well where Meghan was concerned. She already knew that her ability to laugh about it was long gone. And if this tension continued, she was afraid that Westway might be irreparably hurt.

Already the strain was showing in the office, she knew.

The employees realised there was trouble, and it was starting to affect the workers on the production lines and the chemists in the labs—even the salesmen out on the road. They couldn't help but wonder if the difficulty lay within the company itself—if their jobs were safe. She couldn't blame them for being concerned. But the fact was, if this tension wasn't relieved soon, there would be real problems at Westway.

And it's up to me to change it, Gianna thought. I'm the one who's caused the strain, and I'll have to be the one to overcome it. I simply must get along better with Blake, no matter what it takes. I have to make up my mind to the fact that I'm always going to love him, and that he'll never be more than a friend to me. And I have to accept Meghan, if she is his choice, with good grace, because the alternative is to lose him altogether.

'That's easy to say,' she muttered. 'Now how am I going to do it?'

She turned on the rosy bedside lamp and sat up, fluffing the pillows at her back. She reached for the pencil that was always on her night table, ready to note any nocturnal inspirations. She had found long ago that problems were easier to deal with when they were reduced to a single piece of paper; writing things down made them easier to act on. 'It's a little late for New Year resolutions,' she told herself, 'but I suppose it's worth a try.' It was a lead-pipe cinch that she'd better do something about this problem, before it consumed her.

In tiny, precise printing at the top of the page, she wrote, 'I will not say anything negative about Meghan.' She thought about that for a moment, then added, 'I will find one positive thing to say to Blake about her every day.'

Now that, she told herself, ought to be enough of a challenge to keep her mind occupied!

'I will remember to keep my relationship with Blake strictly business,' she wrote. It would be safer that way for a while, she thought. Once she had this awful jealousy licked, perhaps they could be friends again. On a different level, of course, and never again quite as close as they had once been. The realisation that nothing would ever be quite the same made her sad for an instant. She realised, of course, that the same sort of thing happened sooner or later to every friendship. When the friends made other commitments—to husbands, wives, families—the friendship suddenly took second place.

'But that's different,' she mused. 'I expected it with my girl friends, and with the kids I knew in school. But not Blake——' She swallowed hard. There was no sense in even thinking about that.

'I will keep my sense of humour,' she wrote. If she could only learn to laugh about what was happening to her——

'If I manage to do that,' she said sourly, 'I'll be a candidate for immediate sainthood!'

She put the slip of paper on her bedside table, turned the light off, and finally slept. She dreamed of being a bridesmaid at Blake's wedding, walking down the aisle wearing a dress of a particularly hideous mustard yellow that made her look as if she was coming down with jaundice. The dress was too long, and she kept tripping over the hem, falling, and having to pick herself up, gather her flowers back into her basket, and start down the aisle again. In her dream, of course, Meghan was radiant in white satin and pearls, with wisps of orange blossom in her hair. She kept saying to all the guests, 'Isn't Gianna charming? Just a little clumsy, of course, but what else can one expect?'

Gianna woke up before the dream reached the wedding reception. It was just as well, she told herself. She would probably have stabbed Meghan with the cake knife, and it would have been a shame to get bloodstains all over such a beautiful dress.

* * *

Gianna was pouring milk on to her breakfast cereal the next morning when Blake banged on the apartment door. It had to be him, she thought as she put the carton back in the refrigerator. Nobody else ever came to see her at this hour. She noticed that her hands were trembling, just a little. How ridiculous, she told herself. You're acting like a teenager with a silly crush!

Maybe, she thought as she went to answer the door, if I pretend that's all it is, it will go away.

She straightened her shoulders and reminded herself of her resolutions. Now came the hard part, she knew— putting those wonderful ideas into practice for the first time was not going to be easy.

Blake greeted her cheerfully. He was bright-eyed, as if he had looked out at the world this morning and discovered that it suddenly belonged to him.

He's certainly in a good mood, Gianna thought. I wonder if Meghan is the reason.

Don't even think about it, she ordered herself. If Meghan was there in his apartment last night, I don't want to know about it.

And even if Meghan had spent the night with him— well, Gianna told herself firmly, perhaps she was underestimating Meghan. Maybe Megham wasn't really the self-centred, man-chasing, calculating witch that Gianna had assumed her to be. Perhaps she really was the sweet, generous, innocent child that Blake saw——

And if that's true, she told herself, I'll pour my cereal down the drain and eat the bowl instead!

Resolutions, she reminded herself. You're going to find something good to say about Meghan if it kills you.

'What brings you here this morning?' she asked. She tried not to sound ungracious, but she couldn't help the tinge of grumpiness that crept into her voice.

Blake raised an eyebrow. 'What's gotten into you lately? Aren't you getting enough sleep these days?'

'Plenty. If you don't mind coming to the point, I'd like

to get back to my breakfast. My cereal is getting soggy.'

'I could use some coffee myself.'

She debated shutting the door in his face, then yielded. That would scarcely fit with her resolution to put them back on a business like basis, no matter what the cost to her own pride.

He poured himself a mug of coffee and leaned against the kitchen counter to drink it. Gianna perched on a high stool, stirred her soggy cereal, and tried a bite. It was awful.

'This tastes great,' said Blake. 'I haven't had a cup of coffee in three days.'

'Oh? Why not?' As soon as Gianna had said it, she regretted the words.

'Meghan has a thing about caffeine. It's bad for the skin, the nervous system, the stomach—even the heart. She's been after me to give it up, but let me tell you— spring water first thing in the morning just isn't quite the same.' He made a face at the thought.

So Meghan *had* been around in the mornings, had she? Gianna fought a swift battle with her conscience, knowing that it would not be wise to ask questions. She had to bite her tongue so hard that she feared lasting damage, but finally she was able to say, in an almost-normal tone of voice, 'I'm sure Meghan has only your best interests in mind.'

It was lukewarm praise at best, she knew, but it was better than the sharp answer that had been trembling on her tongue. She had almost said, You idiot, if she's making you give up coffee now, wait till you see the agenda after you're married!

She carried the cereal bowl over to the sink and put the contents down the disposal. She felt very proud of herself for not giving in to her baser instincts and screaming at him. 'You haven't told me what you want,' she reminded him.

'I'm on my way to the studio.'

'So what else is new?' she muttered under her breath. She caught herself and thought, So much for resolutions!

Blake looked at her enquiringly, as if he wondered what was bothering her, but he didn't ask. 'Meghan would like the grand tour of Westway,' he told her. 'They'll be finishing in the studio today, I think.'

'That's earlier than you expected, isn't it?'

'Yes. That girl is a real pro in front of the cameras.' His tone was admiring. 'Wait till you see some of the shots we've got!'

Gianna swallowed hard and didn't comment.

'They'll be going out on location for the rest of the week. You know, to shoot the sort of experimental stuff that we'll use in the ad campaigns later in the year.'

'I know.' Gianna was still uncomfortable about spending money on location shooting, until Meghan had proved her worth as an advertising draw. If it had been any other model, at any other time, she would at least have been able to tell him how she felt about it. But there was no sense in arguing with Blake about it.

'I thought I'd bring her out to the plant after the shooting is finished,' he went on, 'so she can see how her perfume is made.'

Her perfume? Gianna mulled over that one for a moment, and decided it wasn't worth arguing about. Blake probably didn't even realise he'd said it that way. 'So bring her out,' she said, with a shrug. 'You certainly don't need my permission.'

'But I won't be there to prepare for her visit.'

'What's to prepare?'

'Well, it gets a bit messy in the plant at times. I hoped you'd do me a favour and get the place in good order. You know, straighten up the offices and make sure we don't have boxes and rejected packages lying around on the production lines——'

'Blake, a certain amount of clutter goes with the territory,' she protested.

'I know that, Gianna, but surely we can straighten the place up a little.'

'Does Meghan also have a thing about neatness?' She caught herself and bit her lip. Well, she thought, there went another resolution down the drain. She murmured, 'Sorry, Blake. The plant does look messy sometimes to a casual visitor. I'll see what I can do.'

'Thanks, hon.' He put his cup in the sink. Beside it was the empty grocery bag, which she had neglected to put away the night before. And under the edge of the bag, Gianna remembered, was the tabloid newspaper she had bought. She gritted her teeth.

Blake picked up the paper. 'I didn't know you read things like this,' he said.

'Every week,' she said flatly. 'I try to conceal it, of course, but it's like an addiction.'

He flipped through the pages, casually. 'Not a very good picture, I don't think.'

'Of what?' She tried not to sound interested.

Blake smiled. 'Of me,' he said. 'On the front page.'

'Are you really?' She reached for the paper. 'Let me see.'

'Are you certain you didn't buy it as a souvenir, Gianna?'

'Why on earth would I?' She inspected the front page as if she had never seen it before. 'You look as if you could use a shave,' she remarked, and handed the newspaper back. 'Have it for your scrapbook, if you like.'

He looked down at the grainy photograph, and then back at her, with an amused gleam in his eyes. He looked like a contented cat, she thought resentfully. It was certainly not the reaction she had expected. Blake had always been a private sort of person, the kind of man who would be upset at the idea of his picture being splashed all over supermarket checkout lanes across the nation.

'You don't seem to mind,' she said, unable to keep silent.

He looked astonished. 'Do you think I should be angry?' He held the newspaper at arm's length. 'What man in his right mind would be upset at this sort of publicity?'

'Well, it should make it easier to get dates in the future.' snapped Gianna, goaded past all endurance. 'Now, I don't want to rush you off, Blake, but I'm already running late, and you've given me a full day's schedule——'

'So you want me to get out of your way?' He switched the coffee pot off.

'Something like that.' She was already reaching for her coat.

'Are you sure you don't want to hang around and talk to me? I've been thinking about a lot of things, and——'

'I can't stay and chat. I have work to do.' It was said stiffly. She thought wearily, there's nothing I'd like to do more than stay here and talk to you, Blake, but you see I know what you want to talk about. And if you mention Meghan's name one more time, I'll throw the toaster at you!

Blake ruffled her hair and smiled down at her, a smile that rocked her heart. 'You're a conscientious soul. You really should take a day off now and then.' He put a casual kiss on her temple. 'You know, Gianna,' he said, as if the thought had just occurred to him, 'my mother may be right after all.'

'About what?' She wanted to rub the spot where his lips had rested. It seemed to be a burning brand on her skin.

'About you making a wonderful wife for someone, some day. We'll see you at the plant this afternoon.'

Gianna stood there motionless, her hands clenched, listening to his cheerful whistle fade across the living-room. He let himself out with a bang of the door, and she bent over the kitchen counter. She felt physically ill. Her head throbbed, her stomach ached, and her whole body felt weak. 'Damn him,' she said painfully. 'Why does he have to make it worse?'

She wanted to crawl back into her bedroom and sleep the day away. But she knew that to lie there in the dim room would only give her time to think. Better to be at the plant, and busy——

'Cleaning up for Meghan!' she groaned.

Traffic was particularly heavy and slow, and by the time she got to the plant, Gianna was in a rare temper. No sooner had she got out of her car than she decided on the first target of her wrath. She had talked to the maintenance people just yesterday about the ice, left over from the last storm, that remained on the main pavement. But today, she noticed indignantly, there were still patches there. They had told her they'd done all they could with sand and salt and hand tools, that unless there was a thaw soon, remnants of ice would continue to plague her. But Gianna was in no mood this morning to be told that she couldn't have what she demanded.

'All I need,' she muttered as she picked her way around the icy spots, 'is for Meghan to fall on that damned sidewalk and break a leg. Then we'd have a lawsuit for damages to her career, to say nothing of the injury to her gorgeous gam. And Blake would probably blame me, since he did ask me to make sure the place was neat.'

She stormed into the office. 'The ice is still on the sidewalk,' she told the secretary flatly.

'I know. The maintenance man worked on it for hours yesterday, after your chat with him. He told me to remind you that this is Chicago, and——'

Gianna glared at her. 'I do know my geography, thank you!'

The secretary sighed. 'All I'm doing is giving you the message, word for word. He said that unless the sun shines and warms the concrete up a few degrees, all the salt in Illinois won't melt the ice off.'

'Then tell him to go home and get his wife's hairdrier

and melt it that way, for heaven's sake! I want that ice off the sidewalk, today, no matter how he has to do it.'

The secretary raised an eyebrow. 'Yes, ma'am,' she said softly, 'I'll tell him.'

It didn't soothe Gianna in the least to know that the secretary thought she was being a little ridiculous. And it only made her more furious to know that by the time she got to the sanctuary of her own office the word would have spread throughout the building that Miss West was in a horrible temper this morning, storm flags were flying and everyone should steer clear of her unless they wanted to be eaten alive . . .

'And tell the janitorial staff to make sure the plant is spit-and-polish this afternoon,' she went on. 'Mr Whittaker is bringing in a special guest.'

As Gianna turned towards her office, the secretary said, 'Miss West——' It was hesitant, as if she debated the wisdom of what she was about to say. 'The article about you is in this morning's paper. I picked it up on the way to work.'

Gianna retraced her steps. 'Thank you. I'm sorry I snapped at you.'

'I understand.'

Gianna wondered bleakly just how much the secretary did understand. More than I'd like, I'm sure, she decided.

She spread the newspaper section out on the table by the windows. 'Unusual that both Blake and I hit the news-stands today,' she muttered. Of course, the circumstances were a little different. Ruthlessly, she dragged her mind off that grainy photograph in the tabloid, and back to the article in front of her.

As she read, a fury began to build deep inside her. The facts were right, but somehow there was a slant to the writing, a twist to the reporter's words that made it appear that Gianna was some sort of idiot who had inherited a company and was pretending to be the boss, all the while refusing to soil her soft white hands with so much as a pencil.

That was bad enough, she thought—making her appear to be some sort of nitwit who didn't know shampoo from eyeliner. For all her careful explanation of the Westway philosophy, it still came out sounding as though she believed that cosmetics were some kind of magic wand to be waved over a woman's head to make her successful.

And as if all that wasn't bad enough, Gianna groaned, the reporter had made her partnership with Blake sound even worse. 'He holds me back,' the story quoted her as saying. The snide twist of the words made it sound as if she thought Blake was incapable of having an idea of any kind, and that she was an irresponsible fool who would run the company into bankruptcy within a week if it wasn't for Blake's strong hand on the reins . . .

She wadded the newspaper up and threw it at the waste-basket. 'That's it,' she said. 'That's the last time I'll ever co-operate with a reporter!'

She thought fleetingly about showing the story to the company's attorney. Perhaps she could sue, and make them take back all the lies—except, she thought, that they really weren't lies. The total effect was false, of course, but it would be very difficult to prove just where the mistaken impressions crossed the line into malice.

No, she decided. Better to let it lie, and learn from the experience.

She dropped into her desk chair and stared at the figures on the green accountant's forms on the blotter. The pages had been lying there since yesterday afternoon, and she was no further along in her anlysis. She couldn't quite see herself getting excited about juggling the numbers for next year's projected sales, when at the moment she didn't even care if Westway sold a single tube of lipstick in the next twelve months. Let Blake worry about it.

But perhaps, she realised, Blake had other plans for his future as well. He had certainly pushed Westway aside in the last couple of weeks, and seemed far more interested in Meghan than in business.

Oh, stop it! she told herself fiercely. Blake had spent countless hours on this campaign, knowing just as well as Gianna how important it was that this new perfume do well. And it was a good product, backed by a good idea. It was only her own jealousy of Meghan—her fear of the woman—that had made Gianna try to back out of the promotional campaign. Even then, weeks ago, she had dimly recognised that Meghan would be the end of everything Gianna had called happiness.

'I was trying to protect myself, then,' she admitted, 'not the company.'

The figures on the page blurred and swam in front of her. She put her head down in her hands and cried. It wasn't fair, she thought, that she had to stick around and put up with this! She hated being so short-tempered and so bitterly unhappy all the time.

And come to that, why should she stay around and wait for the next irritation to hit? She wiped the tears away and sat looking down at the work piled on her desk. She certainly hadn't accomplished much in the last few days, and feeling this way, she wasn't likely to get much done in the near future either. Perhaps a few days away from Westway, away from Blake, away from this awful gloomy weather, would improve her outlook.

'I'll go to Florida,' she said softly. The words had an almost magical effect. She could feel the anger lifting, at the very thought of escaping. She could fly down for a long weekend, at least. She could sleep late, and lie on the beach, play golf with her father, and gossip with her mother——

No, perhaps not that. Carol would probably want to talk about Blake, and that, Gianna decided, would have to be a forbidden subject if she wasn't to come back in worse shape than she was in now. But a few days of sunshine and warmth and play might make all the difference in the world to her attitude. At least, she decided, it was worth a try.

She punched a button on the intercom. 'Get my mother on the line, please,' she told the secretary.

'There's a Mr Elliot on the telephone for you. Would you like to talk to him before I make your other call?'

Gianna frowned. 'Yes, please.' I wonder what he wants, she thought. She hadn't expected him to call. Had the bid he was so sure of fallen through, then? Or perhaps he was calling to tell her that the other people had bought it, so she didn't have to rack her brain over the decision.

Not likely, Gianna thought cynically. If they bought it, he's only calling to gloat—not to put my mind at ease.

She picked up the telephone. 'Yes, Mr Elliot?'

He wasted no time on preliminaries. 'Have you decided whether you want to buy the house I showed you?'

'No. I've scarcely had a chance to think,' she pointed out. 'It was only yesterday afternoon that I went to look at it, if you remember.'

'You certainly sounded impressed with it then.'

'I was. I'm just not sure I want to live in it.' At least, she added to herself, I'm not sure I want to live in it alone, and I don't have any candidates for companionship. 'Could I ask why you're suddenly so anxious for me to make up my mind?' she added.

'Anxious? I'm not anxious. I thought you'd appreciate getting first refusal.'

'Oh? That must mean that your other buyers didn't come through with an offer, after all. Or did the owners want more money?'

Mr Elliot didn't answer. 'Don't wait too long,' he warned. 'They want to sell, and it won't be on the market long.'

'Funny,' commented Gianna, 'but I seem to remember

you telling me yesterday that it was as good as sold.'

'Look,' said Mr Elliot, 'are you interested in making an offer or not?' He sounded irritable.

'I'm not sure,' Gianna said, suddenly serious.

The man sighed. 'You can make any kind of offer you choose—at least it'll give us a place to start negotiating.'

'May I call you back this afternoon?' she asked. 'I'd like an hour or two to think about it.'

Mr Elliot started to protest.

Gianna cut him off in mid-sentence. 'You were so certain yesterday that I wouldn't even have an opportunity to bid,' she said sweetly, 'that I hadn't wasted my time figuring out an amount. I'll talk to you this afternoon.' She put the telephone down with a bang.

'I don't trust that man as far as I can throw him,' she muttered. And yet, if she was to have the house she dreamed of, dealing with Mr Elliot was the only course open to her. Blake would know, she thought. He could sense a crooked deal inside of sixty seconds. And, she had to admit, this one smacked of less-than-honest dealing. Mr Elliot might be a licensed professional, but it was quite possible that he could still be a little shady.

Why had those other people suddenly lost interest in the house, she asked herself suddenly, when they had seemed to be so close to making the purchase? Had they not existed at all, as she had suspected yesterday? Or had they suddenly discovered something wrong with the house? 'The roof might be ready to fall in,' she speculated wildly. 'Or the foundations might be about to collapse.' Heaven knew, she was no expert on either.

Perhaps Blake would go to look at it with me, she thought. He knew all about these things—furnaces and wateL pipes and tiles and so on. He'd know, too, if the price was reasonable, or if Mr Elliot was trying to hold her up.

Her spine straightened. No, she thought, she would not ask Blake. She refused to allow herself to rely on him any more. In the first place, if she did buy the house, she wanted it to be an accomplished fact by the time he discovered she was even thinking about it. She didn't want to have to explain it to him. It was none of his business, after all, whatever she chose to do. If she bought the house, it must be her own decision, based on her own instincts, not on Blake's ideas of what was right for her.

After all, she reminded herself, that was the way she would have to live from now on—for herself, and by herself, and with only herself to rely on.

The figures on the accountant's worksheets were no more intriguing this time around. She stared at them for a while, and then pushed them aside with a sigh. She might as well go out in the plant and make sure everything was falling into place for Meghan's visit.

Her secretary looked up and cupped her hand over the telephone. 'Mrs West's line has been busy,' she said. 'I've just now got through.'

Gianna hurried back to her own office. She'd almost forgotten about asking the secretary to call her mother. 'Hi, Mom,' she said.

'Hello, dear. What makes you call at this odd hour?' Carol sounded a little abstracted.

'How would you like to have company this weekend?'

'You, Gianna? That would be lovely. What's the occasion?'

'I just thought some sunshine would be nice.' It sounded lame, even to her own ears, and she braced herself for the anticipated question.

But if you couldn't have time off at Christmas, Gianna, her mother would ask, why can you suddenly come now? Or she might say, Why don't you bring Blake along? Surely Westway can survive without you both for a few days.

And then, Gianna thought, I don't know what I'm going to say. But I'm awfully afraid I'll start crying, and spill everything out over the phone——

Instead, Carol said, 'That will be wonderful, dear. What time will you be arriving?'

'I don't know, I haven't got my ticket yet.'

There ws a split-second pause on the other end of the line, then Carol said, 'Let us know when to meet you, Gianna. I'm sorry to cut you off like this, but we're playing bridge this morning, and the table is waiting for me.'

'Sure, Mom. Goodbye.' Gianna put the telephone down gently.

You should be pleased she didn't ask questions, she told herself. You should be delighted you didn't have to explain this sudden decision.

But she didn't feel particularly pleased. She felt alone, as if everyone in the world had suddenly deserted her.

CHAPTER TEN

GIANNA SELDOM spent much time in the factory itself. The president of the company belonged in the front office managing the business, she remembered her father saying more than once, not in the plant watching every move on the production line. His philosophy was to hire a capable employee, then stand aside so the employee could do the job. It made sense to Gianna, so she too had always made it a point not to hover over the factory superintendent.

Yet the production line was one of her favourite places. She loved to find a quiet corner and watch as the giant mixers kneaded ingredients together to produce the heavy-bodied facial mask. The huge blades whined at an ever-increasing pitch as the mixture thickened, and an experienced ear could tell precisely when the batch was done, without even glancing at the sophisticated equipment that measured the process.

She slowly descended the stairs to the packing and shipping lines, careful of the slender high heels of her shoes on the steel grating of the steps. She made a mental note to notice what kind of shoes Meghan was wearing, and warn Blake to make sure his guest didn't twist an ankle on the steps.

'And what makes you think he needs to be warned?' she muttered to herself. 'He probably won't let go of her arm for an instant!'

The packing department was much quieter. The only noise here was of the machines that automatically filled each jar or bottle with a pre-set amount of cleansing cream, or astringent, or whatever other product was being stockpiled. Beside each machine a woman sat on a high stool, unpacking empty blue and gold Westway containers from a crate and feeding them into the machine. On the other end, several workers inspected each full container, setting aside a faulty one now and then, before the caps were put on and the finished products were packed back into boxes to be shipped to distributors around the country. Every one of the workers wore paper masks and plastic gloves, and even the air was carefully filtered and re-filtered to prevent any possibility of contamination.

At the far end of the room, behind a glass partition, the perfume department was working full-speed to produce and bottle enough crystal flagons of *Sensually Meghan* to meet the initial demand. Gianna didn't even want to go back there today. Even though the machinery was designed to let no fragrance escape, even a whiff of that scent today would be enough to make her ill, she thought. So she stayed safely on the cosmetics side.

She picked up one of the cast-aside jars. It had slipped out of position inside the machine, and the nozzle had struck the edge of the jar instead of precisely in the middle. Aromatic cleansing cream was piled on top of the rim like whipped topping on a hot fudge sundae, but fully half the cream that was supposed to be in the jar had oozed down over the side instead and formed a thick puddle on the conveyor belt.

I wonder, Gianna thought as she stood there with the messy jar in her hand, how many empty Westway containers are thrown away every day.

The blue and gold containers were practical, there was no doubt about that. And they were attractive, up to a point. But what if we could produce an élite line? she wondered. The same products, but in a more elegant container that women would be proud to display on any dressing table, and that they could refill and keep. Something that looks more like crystal, perhaps, she decided—like the perfume bottles we already use. We could keep the Westway blue and gold on the lid, and perhaps dress it up with a little filigree design. But the only identification would be the label on the bottom of the jar.

She made a mental note to mention it to Blake. Such a container would cost more, but it would also allow them to produce a new gift set that might take off in the Christmas market next year.

She wondered if Blake would even sit still to listen, or if he was so absorbed in Meghan's perfume right now that the regular cosmetics lines had lost all interest for him.

Then she was irritated at her own readiness to jump to conclusions. Just because Blake was obviously attracted to Meghan it didn't mean that he was automatically going to ditch his own career, even if he ended up marrying her.

At least he'd better not, Gianna thought, given the odds of survival that a marriage of that sort would have.

Enough, she told herself testily. She hadn't come out here to stand and speculate about Blake's plans for getting married. After all, she realised, she was only guessing that he intended to do anything of the sort. Blake had said nothing about marriage. And even if he did propose, there was no certainty that Meghan would accept.

She'd have to be an idiot to turn him down, Gianna told herself. Blake was a man in a million—warm and loving, affectionate, charming.

Also stubborn, exasperating, and too darn good at gin rummy, she added. And it would be wise to remember all his irritating characteristics, just so you don't start thinking that he's some kind of a saint.

At any rate, he couldn't have any plans to marry Meghan. Just a couple of weeks ago, her traitorous heart reminded her, he had proposed to Gianna herself.

'But only so he'd always have a date to the next big party,' she muttered.

'Miss West?' The woman beside her stopped setting jars into the box at her elbow. She looked startled. 'Did you say something?'

Gianna felt like a fool. 'Oh, it was nothing.' She gestured with the half-full jar she held. 'Does this happen often?'

The woman shook her head. 'No. There's nothing wrong with the machine, but one jar in every thousand or so slips a little out of position.'

Gianna nodded and set the jar carefully back in the tray of discards. Idiot, she accused herself. Standing there in the middle of the factory talking to yourself! And about Blake, of all things. It's time for you to go back to your office, where at least no one will hear you going quietly berserk!

She retreated to the office end of the building, and told her secretary to hold all her telephone calls. 'I'm working on the sales projections,' she said, 'and heaven knows I don't need any distractions.' The secretary nodded, and Gianna closed the heavy door of her office behind her with a sense of relief. But she didn't sit down at her desk. Instead, she walked over to the long windows that faced the car park.

She tried to think of other things—to plot out her day's work, to plan for the weekend—but those joking proposals of Blake's, once allowed into her mind, refused to retreat. 'Marry me,' he had said, 'and you'll always have someone handy to zip up your dress.'

I should have been smart enough to jump at the chance, she thought. How could I have been so dumb as not to see that he was what I really wanted?

Oh, don't be ridiculous, Gianna, she told herself gloomily. You're acting as if he was serious about that proposal. It was only a joke to him. He said himself that if you ever said yes he'd die of shock. Unpleasant shock, at that.

She mopped a tear away, then got angry because she was feeling sorry for herself. It would have served Blake right, she thought, if she *had* accepted his proposal, and immediately called up everyone they knew to announce the happy news, and then watched him try to squirm out of the mess! If I ever have another chance, she decided, I'll do it.

She lost herself for a moment in pleasant dreams of the storm it would cause. Then she shook herself back to common sense. She couldn't do it, because it would cause her too much pain. It would be too hard to pretend it didn't matter, once the game was over.

If only things had been different, she thought dreamily. If only he had said, 'Marry me, Gianna. I'm wild about you. I can't live without you . . .'

She smiled just a little, thinking about that. She knew his voice so well that she could actually hear how the words would sound, just a little husky, with an undertone of passion . . .

Dreamer, she accused herself baldly. She ought to know better than to do this—to pretend that she was anything to him except a troublesome younger sister, a tag-along nuisance who always needed something fixed. All she was accomplishing was to make herself hurt worse.

She leaned against the window frame, the cold of the glass chilling her cheek, the rough texture of the curtain teasing her skin. But not even the harshness of those sensations could keep away the gentle memories of the way Blake had kissed her. The warmth of the fire on Christmas Eve, as they had relaxed beside it—the feel of his mouth gentle against hers . . .

She closed her eyes and sighed, remembering. Then she pulled herself back to reality. There was no sense standing here by the window daydreaming, she told herself abruptly. Thinking about it certainly didn't change the fact that what had happened on Christmas Eve had been only a friendly, casual kiss that had got out of hand. And if she ever let herself forget that, she would be in real trouble.

She went back to her desk, determined to lunge into the accountant's figures. The projections would have to be anlysed before she went to Florida, she told herself. She selected an apple from the basket on the corner of her desk and bit into it. Then, just as she picked up her finely sharpened pencil, the intercom buzzed.

'I thought I said to hold all my calls,' she told the secretary, with a bit of irritation.

'It's Mrs Whittaker, calling about lunch today. I thought you'd want to talk to her——'

Well, that was reasonable enough, Gianna thought. Except that she hadn't arranged a lunch date with Gwen. She sighed. How was the secretary to know that? 'All right,' she said. 'And by the way, would you call the airlines and see if you can book a seat to Fort Lauderdale for me on Friday?' She didn't wait for an answer. She punched the telephone button with the eraser on her pencil and said, 'Good morning, Gwen.'

'Hello, dear. It's awfully short notice, I know, but a friend of mine had two tickets for the fashion show luncheon at the mall today, and she woke up with a dreadful head cold and can't use them. Would you like to go with me?'

Gianna hesitated. What pleasant excuse could she use? she wondered. She didn't want to hurt Gwen's feelings, and though she was certain that Gwen understood the press of business, she hated to leave her in the lurch. It was no fun to go to a fashion show alone. But Gianna just didn't feel quite right about going to lunch today with Blake's mother——

Then her heart rebelled. Why shouldn't I go? she asked herself. Gwen isn't only Blake's mother, she's my friend. Why should I be cheated out of her friendship just because Blake and I aren't on the best of terms these days?

She looked down at the worksheets spread across her desk. Perhaps a little recreation, and a break from this awful gloom, she felt, would help her to concentrate later. I still have tomorrow to work on it, she thought. And I'll stay till midnight if I must.

'Shall I pick you up?' she heard herself asking.

'That would be wonderful. Fifteen minutes?'

'Sure. I'm not exactly dressed for a fashion show,' Gianna warned.

Gwen's laugh bubbled. 'Oh, if I expected you to be in it, I'd have given you at least an hour's notice!'

When Gianna knocked at the front door of the Whittaker house, Gwen was just putting on her fur jacket. 'Darn!' she muttered. 'I can't remember where I left my hat. I'll have to run upstairs and check in my closet.'

Gianna wandered into the big living-room. Boxes were scattered over the floor, and bits of tinsel were tangled into the fibres of the carpet. The tree, half denuded of its glittery decorations, looked pathetic and old in the light of day. No more magic or mystery now, Gianna thought sadly. All that was over for another year.

And for some of us, she thought, it might just be over for ever. Never again would Christmas be quite the same for her, that was certain.

She caught herself staring at the empty hearth, recreating those mad moments of Christmas Eve in her mind, and forced herself to stop. She turned her back on the fireplace, and saw that on the table the Christmas album was laid out, with the pages open to this year's celebration. They were empty still, except for the date at the top of the page.

And what would Gwen write here, she wondered, to be read on futute holidays? She should label this as the last Christmas Blake and Gianna were friends, Gianna thought sadly. With any luck, though, Gwen would never need to know that . . .

And just what kind of a dreamer was she, to believe that Gwen wouldn't notice? She turned the pages slowly back, erasing time and years.

'I found it!' Gwen's voice was triumphant. She came in, settling a tiny fur hat on her silver hair. 'I see you discovered my guilty secret. I hate taking the decorations down, so any temptation that comes along is enough to make me quit the job.'

Gianna smiled. It sounded very familiar.

'You wouldn't want to take over the chore of keeping up the Christmas album, would you?' asked Gwen.

Gianna shook her head and released the pages. 'It's a Whittaker family tradition,' she pointed out.

Gwen shrugged. 'Who keeps track? And you must know, Gianna, that Hal and I have always hoped that some day you'd really be our daughter——'

So here it was, finally out in the open. And what can I say? Gianna asked herself. If Gwen had said those same words a month ago I'd have laughed at the very idea. Now, I only want to throw myself in her arms and cry about how much I love him. I must disillusion her, before she's hurt worse. But what can I say? Telling her about Meghan wouldn't be fair to Blake. If there was an announcement to be made, Blake would have to make it, when he was ready.

'Gwen, I don't think you and I should talk about this——' Her voice was husky. I know I can't talk about it, she thought, in sudden panic. I'll break down and wail like a baby in another minute.

'Of course I understand,' said Gwen, in her mother-hen tone. 'I promised I wouldn't pester you about it, and I won't. Not another word, I swear.'

She put a gentle arm about Gianna's shoulders. 'Now we can't let them start the fashion show without us, can we?'

I'd be delighted to skip it, Gianna thought, if it meant I could climb into a cave somewhere and never come out again. If only I never had to face Gwen, or Mother—or Blake—again . . .

But I couldn't bear that, she thought. Never again to share with him that delicious sense of the ridiculous? Never to see that beloved smile again?

No, she thought. Any amount of pain was bearable, so

long as she could see him. So long as she had some part, however small, in his life.

She had been back in her office only a few minutes when a tap on her door gave her an excuse to put her pencil down. Blake looked in. 'Sorry to disturb you,' he said, with a smile that made her heart tingle, 'but I've been searching everywhere for the mock-ups of the ad campaign——'

'They're locked in my safe,' Gianna said briefly. She tried to turn back to the figures on the green worksheets, but there was no point. She had only been pretending to work, anyway. She watched him covertly as he spun the combination lock with long strong fingers.

You should ignore him, she told herself firmly. You'll only hurt yourself more by brooding over forbidden fruit.

But it didn't work. She watched him anyway, and remembered the way those strong fingers had caressed her.

He looked up, with the plans in his hand, and said, 'Would you mind if I bring them in here to look at these?'

'Them?' she queried.

'Meghan and Curtis.'

She merely nodded. What difference did it make? She hadn't seen them together since New Year's Eve, but she couldn't put it off for ever. Perhaps it would be better to get it over now, instead of waiting for the inevitable moment when she would run into Meghan outside his apartment. It was probably a miracle that it hadn't happened already.

I want to move, Gianna told herself firmly, and remembered that she had not yet called Mr Elliot back. I'll do that as soon as the crowd clears out of my office, she decided. And I won't be touchy about the price, either. Her mind was made up now; it would be worth any amount of money to be able to move right away.

The secretary ushered Meghan and Curtis in, and Gianna murmured to her, 'Remind me to call Mr Elliot this afternoon, please.'

'Mr Elliot?' the secretary asked. She sounded a little puzzled. 'Do I have the number?'

Gianna shook her head. 'Just don't let me forget. It's very important that I reach him today.'

'Elliot?' asked Blake. 'What kind of a deal do you have going now, Gianna?'

She told herself there were hundreds of people in the city who were named Elliot, and that it was only her morbid imagination that made her think Blake might know this particular one. 'It's nothing that concerns Westway, Blake.'

He raised an eyebrow at the tone of her voice. 'If he's a stockbroker,' he said mildly, 'don't gamble your life savings. The market's going to go down.'

'Thanks for the benefit of your experience,' Gianna said tartly. But she was relieved. For one awful moment, she had suspected that Blake might have been reading her mind! She was grateful that he hadn't pushed. There would be plenty of time for explanations after the deal was struck.

'Think nothing of it.' He spread the mock-ups out on the table and turned his attention to Meghan, who inspected each ad enthusiastically.

Gone was the false modesty that had so irritated Gianna when she first met the model. Now the girl was showing delight with each photograph, each idea, each pose.

The modesty must have only been a front she uses to get a man's attention, Gianna thought. Well, it had certainly worked on Blake. He was standing very close to Meghan, pointing out a detail here and there, and the model was looking up at him in wide-eyed wonder.

With difficulty, Gianna pulled her gaze away from the pair at the table and met Curtis's eyes. He had glanced through the layouts, nodded an abrupt approval, and gone to sit down, tapping his foot and glancing now and then at his watch. She felt a little sorry for him, actually. The man must spend the greater part of his life waiting—

watching while photographs were taken, or biding his time while Meghan was groomed and dressed and made ready. And even though he was probably paid very well, it must get dull sometimes. Did all models have managers do this sort of thing? she wondered. Or was Curtis unusual in his devotion to Meghan's career?

Most models probably couldn't afford to have a Curtis waiting in the wings, she decided. But Meghan could no doubt hire as many as she wanted.

Gianna's eyes rested thoughtfully on Blake's broad shoulders. Was that what Meghan had in mind? And was that why Curtis was so nervous—because he sensed, or knew, that he might not be Meghan's main adviser for much longer?

Quit it, Gianna ordered herself, and get yourself to Florida for a vacation as soon as you can. You're getting paranoid!

'Meghan,' Curtis reminded her gently, 'we have a plane to catch.'

The model nodded over her shoulder, not taking her eyes off Blake's face.

'You're leaving for location already?' Gianna asked. Not that she cared, exactly, she thought, but any kind of conversation was better than listening to the murmur of voices from the table.

Curtis nodded. 'If we travel this afternoon, we've got two full days left to shoot.'

'I thought you'd take a day off, at least.'

'When we work, we work—as many hours as the job requires.'

'Where are you going?' she asked.

'Southern California. It's not Meghan's favourite place to shoot, but we can rely on the weather. And her next job is there, anyway, so we can squeeze out a little more time for Westway.'

'I'm sure Meghan has more work than she can handle,' said Gianna tartly.

'That's right. Meghan honey, let's get this show on the

road. If you want to see the perfume made, let's go see it
now.'

Meghan looked at him with big, sad eyes, but she
didn't protest.

I don't blame her, Gianna thought. She doesn't want to
leave Blake, any more than I would.

'You've been nagging me for three days to get you out
of the cold before it damaged your skin,' Curtis went on,
in a softer tone. 'Let's not miss the chance.'

Blake had looked at his watch. 'I'm sorry, Curtis,' he
said. 'It's later than I thought. I'll take you out to the
factory now.'

'Enjoy your tour,' said Gianna, feeling as if she was
waving off a group of schoolchildren on a field trip.

'Come along if you like, Gianna,' Blake invited.

And feel like an intruder? She shook her head. 'I'm
working on next year's projections,' she told him. It was
only half a lie, she told herself; she should be working on
them. 'And I want to complete the job before I leave this
weekend.' Why did she feel as if she was apologising? she
wondered angrily.

His eyebrows raised. 'Oh? Where are you planning to
go?'

'What business is it of yours? Away, that's all.' She was
darned if she would explain to Blake where she spent her
weekends, and with whom!

'You're not leaving till Saturday, I hope.'

She looked up in surprise. 'Are you telling me I can't
take a day off?'

'That's the general idea. I've scheduled some
things——'

She flung her pencil down. 'I don't believe it! After
you've spent the better part of the last two weeks out of
the office——'

'That was different.'

'Oh, of course it was!' Her voice was heavy with
sarcasm. 'Your tour is waiting for you,' she pointed out.
'Why don't you run along now and let me get my work

done? Because, you see, I'm leaving on Friday, regardless of what you say.' She bent her head over the worksheets again, her hand sheltering her eyes.

Blake looked at her grimly. 'I'm going to take Meghan and Curtis on their tour,' he said. 'I'll be back to continue this discussion.'

'Unfortunately for me,' Gianna muttered, 'I'm sure you will.'

She didn't expect him for an hour or two. It would take that long, she thought, to answer all Meghan's questions. By then, Gianna hoped, she herself would have cooled off somewhat.

But she didn't have the chance.

Less than fifteen minutes later he was back in her office. The brief interlude had not re-established her calm; instead, it had made her even angrier. How dared he give her orders! she thought. They had always shared those decisions. She wasn't used to being dictated to.

She whirled to face him. 'Well, that didn't take long!'

'I turned the tour over to the factory supervisor.' He didn't sound very happy about it. Gianna wasn't surprised.

'I suppose I should feel grateful that you considered our talk more important!' she snapped, fury threatening to burn up her voice. 'I don't know what makes you think you set the rules around here, all of a sudden. You've been gone for days, playing chauffeur and prince consort to Meghan! Now I want one day off and you tell me I can't have it, as if you had any right to dictate to me!'

'Gianna,' he began. 'I'm sorry if I sounded like a dictator——'

'You certainly did!' She refused to be soothed. 'I suppose you want me to stay because you're intending to go out on location with her!'

'I don't see why you should be surprised,' he said mildly. 'We're paying her five thousand dollars a day modelling fees, on top of the fee for the use of her name. I'd like to be sure we're getting our money's worth.'

Gianna pounced. 'Do you really expect me to believe that? It's got nothing to do with money, and you know it. You've been living in her pocket for two weeks, and ignoring the rest of the business——'

'I have not ignored Westway,' he corrected.

'Well, you've been giving a good imitation of it! Dammit, Blake, I understand that you're head over heels in love with her. It could happen to any man, but that's no excuse. All I want is one day off——'

'Well, you can't have Friday. I scheduled that talk show for then, and you have to be there.'

Another reporter? Not on your life, she thought. Not after what the last one did to me. 'Why should I?' she snapped. 'So you and Meghan can be free to frolic in the surf in Southern California? Forget it, Blake. You scheduled it, and you can unschedule it!'

The intercom buzzer sounded, and the secretary said, 'Mr Whittaker, your guests are waiting.'

He ignored it.

Gianna said tartly, 'You'd better run, or you might miss your plane.'

Blake gave no evidence of having heard her. He started walking towards her, slowly. Very softly he said, 'Gianna, are you so angry because you're jealous of the attention Meghan's getting?'

Gianna gave a sharp laugh. 'Jealous of Meghan? Don't be ridiculous, Blake!' Her heart was pounding. Stop there, she pleaded silently. Don't wonder any more, Blake—I can't stand to have you feel sorry for me.

'If it isn't all the fuss over her that's causing the problem, then what are you jealous of?' He was only a step from her, now.

'I never said I was jealous at all,' Gianna parried. She backed away a little.

She was breathing hard, and trying to hide it from him. I'm so jealous of Meghan, she thought, that my heart is cracking right now because it can't hold all the jealousy I feel. I'm not envious of her beauty, or her fame, or her talent, or her wealth. I only envy her you, Blake. What I wouldn't give to have you defending me like this!

She felt the cool hardness of the wall at her back, and could not remember making the slow retreat across the room. She looked up into hazel eyes, fearful of what she would see there.

'Gianna——' It was a husky whisper. His lips brushed hers, a mere breath of a kiss, a butterfly caress. For an instant, she stood stock still, wanting desperately to press herself against him until her muscles melted into his, until she became a part of him, until her will submitted itself entirely to him.

But that, she realised hazily, must be what he expected to happen. He thought she would give in, if he kissed her into submission. He could leave her, then, to do the talk show as he wanted, while he went merrily off to California with Meghan. It was all right for him to use whatever methods worked, he thought, because he was the boss. Well, I'll show him what I think of that! Gianna decided.

She gathered the frayed strands of her pride. 'If you ever do that again,' she said icily, 'I'll scream the roof down. Now, Meghan is waiting for you, and I have work to do.'

She stepped around him carefully, and went to her desk. Her hands were trembling. She tried to still them by clutching the arms of her chair.

He looked astounded, she thought, as if his favourite puppy had suddenly nipped his fingers.

Well, perhaps that's the way he's always looked at me, she thought wearily. A pet of a sort, there to please him, and do as he told me. But no more.

'Is that all you wanted to say?' Blake asked quietly.

'Not quite.' Gianna looked up at him steadily, and kept her voice level with an effort. 'I've had it with these stupid, sexist games. From now on, Blake, it's to be strictly business—nothing more. You're the Chairman of the board, and I'm the President—and that's all. Got it?'

His eyes had gone black with anger, and she felt fear tingle up her spine. His jaw twitched just a little. But he didn't say a word. He stood there and stared down at her for a moment, then he strode towards the door and slammed it behind him.

Gianna sank back weakly into her chair. She was suddenly cold, and her muscles didn't seem to want to co-operate. She was like a puppet unstrung by a careless child.

I have to get out of here, she thought. Blake never quits anything until he's satisfied, and if he comes back——I can't take that, she thought. Not right now.

She got her coat from the closet and took her car keys from her handbag. She would try, she decided, to slip out of the building while he was still in his office with Curtis and Meghan. There would be a reckoning later, she knew; there always was, with Blake. But at the moment all that mattered was escape.

What she hadn't expected was that the three of them would be standing in the main office, behind the desk where the secretary sat. Gianna's eyes widened in shock, but then she realised that none of them was paying her any attention at all. As she watched, Blake said, 'I'll see you both later, then.' He put an arm around Meghan's shoulders and drew her close for a kiss on the cheek.

So what did you expect? Gianna asked herself drearily. Why should he try to keep it secret? Everyone has always known he's in love with her. The whole country knows it now.

And he was putting Meghan off, so he could settle this quarrel with Gianna—— Escape seemed suddenly even more important.

She caught her secretary's eye, touched her finger to her lips, and made elaborate motions towards the door. The secretary frowned, then said, 'Miss West, you wanted me to remind you to make that telephone call this afternoon——'

The trio turned. Blake took two steps towards her, and

Gianna pushed the door open and fled. I'd like to fire that girl! she raged as she ran towards her car. She has no common sense whatever——

She saw the patch of ice on the pavement in the split second before her toe came to rest on it, and time seemed to draw out endlessly as her shoe skidded on the glossy surface. For the long moment that she was airborne, scrambling to save herself, gravity itself seemed to have taken a vacation.

Then the heart-stopping moment was over, and the pavement rose up to greet her. She met it with a thump that knocked the wind out of her lungs, and with an awful, sharp crack that seemed to come from her right wrist, trapped under her against the concrete.

CHAPTER ELEVEN

'GIANNA, don't move!' Blake shouted the order from half-way down the sidewalk.

'You don't need to scream at me.' Warily she shifted her weight, trying to assess the damage.

'Lie still, dammit,' he ordered. 'The way you went down, you could have broken anything—or everything, for that matter.'

'No, it's only my wrist.'

His face was pale as he knelt over her. That was funny, she thought. Why should he have turned white? She was the one who had taken the tumble. Or did he feel that he was to blame? She hoped he did; after all, it was because of him that she had been running.

'Could you raise me up so I can get my hand free?' she asked.

'I'd rather wait till the nurse gets here.'

'Blake, don't be ridiculous. All I did was sprain my wrist!'

'No other pain?' His fingers were gentle as he smoothed a stray lock of hair back from her temple.

The gesture brought tears to her eyes, but she shook them away. He'd probably prefer to sock me in the jaw, she thought, if only his mother hadn't taught him to be a gentleman!

She shook her head. 'Oh, I've been reminded that I have a tailbone, but that's only to be expected, wouldn't you say?'

'Nevertheless, you're staying right there for the present.' He looked anxiously towards the building.

No doubt, she thought, he was concerned that Meghan might be getting the wrong idea. She took advantage of his preoccupation and rolled over a little, just enough to free her hand. As she moved it, pain stabbed up through her arm. Beads of sweat broke out on her face.

'Gianna, I told you to lie still!' He sounded angry.

Well, that was nothing new. 'If you'll just help me get up——'

'I'm not helping you to do anything. The nurse is on her way.'

'Blake, it's cold down here. Do you want me to catch pneumonia?' Probably, she thought drearily. She wanted to cry, but she refused to give in.

'You should have thought of that before you came running out here in those shoes. I've never seen anything less sensible in my life.'

'It wasn't the fault of the shoes,' snapped Gianna, forgetting for a moment that she was still lying on a slab of cold concrete. 'I wish you'd stop yelling at me about my shoes!'

'Oh? Do you mean you walked out here on your elbows?'

'It was the patch of ice I told them to remove——' If it had been Meghan who had fallen, she thought, he wouldn't have been sarcastic about her shoes. He'd have been telling her what a wonderful girl she was for not getting upset!

'Four-inch heels aren't a sensible choice for this time of year,' he observed. 'However, there's no point in arguing about your shoes.'

'That's right. I'm glad you realise that what I put on my feet is none of your concern.'

Blake went on blandly, 'Because you won't be wearing this pair again.' He displayed one slender heel, twisted and scuffed, which had snapped off from the shoe.

Gianna wailed, 'Those were brand new! I paid two hundred and ten dollars for those shoes——'

Blake inspected the heel and tossed it aside. 'You were robbed.'

The nurse who had been on call in the plant's first-aid room arrived, and Blake moved aside. 'Am I ever glad to see you!' Gianna told her. 'The self-appointed Red Cross expert over there wouldn't even let me move.

'Well, neither will I until I'm sure you won't be doing more damage.' The nurse's hands were busy. 'Any pain here? Or here?'

Gianna shook her head. 'Just my wrist. I must have sprained it.'

'I've already heard about it. If I was betting, I'd say you've fractured it. That's why I brought a splint with me—just in case.'

'That's ridiculous! See? I can move it——' Gianna had forgotten how much it had hurt to try to bend the wrist, and she couldn't quite swallow her moan of pain.

'Don't you dare do that again!' ordered Blake.

'Don't bellow at me!' Gianna snapped. 'When did you get your commission in the Marines?'

The nurse slid an inflatable splint under Gianna's arm and fastened it. She worked quickly and steadily, as if unaware of the argument raging around her. Blake was pacing back and forth on the sidewalk.

'Go away,' Gianna told him. 'I certainly wouldn't want you to miss that plane.'

'Well, obviously you didn't break anything in your mouth,' Blake retorted.

The nurse interrupted. 'Any pain in your legs, Miss West? Or your back?'

Gianna shook her head. 'Only my tailbone,' she said. 'And even that's not nearly as much of a pain as he is.' She nodded towards Blake.

The nurse looked at her speculatively a moment. 'I don't think it's necessary to wait for an ambulance,' she said.

'Well, that's a blessing,' Gianna said wryly. 'I suppose you're going to insist that I have my wrist X-rayed.'

The nurse ignored her. 'If we lift her carefully, I think

you can drive her to the hospital, Mr Whittaker,' she said. 'The wrist is immobilised now.'

'I can lift myself, thank you,' said Gianna with dignity. 'And I can drive myself to the hospital, too.'

'You're not going to try,' Blake said grimly.

'What's the matter? Are you afraid I'll crack up my car?'

'No. I'm worried about the safety of every other driver on the streets.' He bent over her. 'Curtis, give me a hand, will you?'

'I'm not that heavy,' Gianna said spitefully.

'Put your arms around my neck.' They raised her off the sidewalk, and suddenly she was cradled in Blake's arms, the unwieldy plastic splint preventing her from helping to support herself. It was rather nice, she thought. Secure, and warm, and a whole lot more comfortable than the concrete, with the scent of his favourite after-shave tickling her nose, where it rested against his warm shoulder.

And that's enough of that, she told herself, swallowing the lump in her throat. Time to bring such dangerous reflections to a close, and to remember that he would never hold her this way again. 'Don't drop me,' she said.

'Don't tempt me,' warned Blake. He strode over to his car, and Curtis opened the passenger door. Blake set Gianna in, shut the door, and stood for a moment talking to Curtis. They both looked serious, as if the discussion didn't please either of them. Of course, Gianna thought miserably. Her accident had thrown a wrench into everyone's plans.

Well, I couldn't help it, she reminded herself. If he hadn't been set on persuading me with physical means, I wouldn't have gone tearing out of the building in such a hurry. Why he ever thought that kissing me would make me do as he wanted——

It brought back the memory of that featherlight caress, and she shivered. I'd do anything he wanted, she admitted to herself. That was why I ran—because I was afraid of what I'd say to him if he came back.

The men shook hands, and Blake waved across the frozen lawn to Meghan, who was standing inside the building, watching. That was typical, Gianna thought cattily. She wouldn't come outside because the cold air might injure her skin. What in heaven's name Blake saw in that woman was beyond her——

Then she looked down at the splint on her wrist, and the dirt embedded in the palm of her hand where she had scraped it on the pavement. I know what he sees in Meghan, she thought. She never reminds him of a troublesome little sister.

When he came around the car and slid behind the wheel, she said meekly, 'You don't have to stay with me, Blake. Someone else can take me to the hospital.'

'I don't trust anyone else to get you there,' he said absently. 'Especially when you don't want to go.'

'Blake, I promise I'll have the wrist taken care of. Just go on and catch your plane——'

He turned towards her for a moment. His eyes were cold. 'Look, Gianna,' he said, 'I know quite well that you don't want me around; you've made that very plain. But you aren't getting rid of me, so you might as well shut up.' He put the car into gear with a jerk.

That wasn't what I meant at all, she thought. It isn't that I don't want him around; I want him too much. But the silence inside the car was so stiff that she didn't even try to explain what she had meant. What was the use?

She had never heard him sound so brusque—not to her, at least. Gone was the humour, the teasing and cajoling, that he had always used to get his way. Even friendship, Gianna thought, was beyond their reach now. I can only go half-way, she thought. If he doesn't want to compromise, there's nothing more I can do.

But hadn't she been the one who had put an end to the possibility of friendship? Strictly business, she had said it was to be from now on . . .

The nearest suburban hospital was a small one. When Blake turned the car into the emergency entrance, Gianna protested once more. 'I can walk in by myself, for heaven's sake.'

The look he gave her was enough to silence her once more. At the emergency entrance, an orderly appeared with a wheelchair. Gianna considered arguing about it, then gave in. Considering the sort of mood Blake was in at the moment, anything might happen. Besides, she thought, she'd forgotten that she only had one complete shoe.

But why should Blake be so angry? she thought as the orderly wheeled her into a cubicle off the main corridor of the emergency room. It wasn't like him to be so upset, even when his plans were abruptly interrupted.

'I wish he'd just go to California and never come back,' she muttered.

Long minutes later, she found herself wondering if he had done just that. He must have gone to park the car in the ramp, she thought, so it didn't block the emergency entrance. But how long could that take? Gianna wondered fretfully. Where was he? Her head was beginning to hurt. It was the tension of the day, not an injury, she thought; at least she couldn't remember banging her head on the pavement.

The X-rays had been taken and she was back in her cubicle, lying on the examining table, by the time Blake showed up. She had been shocked to realise, when they removed the temporary splint, that her wrist had swollen. Already bruises were beginning to show on her fair skin.

'I'm going to be miserable tomorrow,' she muttered, remembering the way she had slammed into the concrete.

'No more than you deserve,' said Blake unsympathetically from the doorway. 'You were running down an icy pavement as if there was a bull after you!'

Tears sprang to her eyes. 'Don't be mean to me,' she begged. 'I can't stand it when you're mean to me.'

He came across the room quietly and stood beside her, stroking her forehead with gentle fingers. Gianna tried to turn her head away, to hide the blistering tears that seeped from the corner of her eye and trickled down her temple before losing themselves in her hair.

He stooped over her, and Gianna almost stopped breathing. Is he going to kiss me? she wondered. Her throat was so tight she could't have made a sound.

He straightened up abruptly, as a white-coated woman came in. 'Miss West?' she said.

For a moment, Gianna almost didn't hear her. She was lost in longing for what might have been, wishing the doctor hadn't chosen that particular moment to inter-rupt. Then reason reasserted itself. Interrupt what? she asked herself. It was only her own imagination that insisted Blake had intended to kiss her. Common sense said the opposite. What was it she had told him in her office earlier? Something about screaming the roof down if he ever touched her again.

Well, she told herself drearily, you can rest easy on that question. After this whole mess, he'll never want to touch you again.

Neither of them had said a word, all the way from the hospital across town to the high-rise beside the lake. Gianna looked down at the pristine white cast that encased her arm from knuckles to elbow, and groaned silently. Six weeks, the doctor had said. A month and a half of hauling this appendage around before she would be back to normal.

The doorman exclaimed when they came through the lobby. I must be quite a sight, Gianna thought gloomily. Her hair was hanging untidily around her face. Her coat was awkwardly draped around her, over the sling that protected the bulky plaster cast.

At least my shoes match again, she thought. Blake had wrenched the heel off the other shoe so she could walk, but the result wasn't precisely comfortable. I don't think it will catch on as a new fashion, she told herself.

She didn't explain anything to the doorman. Let him wonder, she thought. Whatever story he concocts, it will be better than the truth.

At her apartment door, she fumbled with her key, and only then began to realise how very inconvenient it was going to be, without the full use of her right hand for the next six weeks.

Blake took the key and opened the door. 'Go lie down,' he ordered.

Gianna kicked off the wreckage of her expensive shoes and dropped them in the nearest waste-basket, then went without complaint to the couch. Every bone in her body seemed to be protesting at the rough treatment.

She was lying with her good arm over her eyes when Blake came in from the kitchen a moment later. 'Here's your painkiller,' he said.

She sat up obediently and swallowed the tablet.

'What would you like for dinner?' he asked.

'Nothing.' She turned her face away. 'You don't have to stay here and play nursemaid, Blake.'

'The doctor said you might be in pain tonight.'

'So? I can be in pain alone.' In any case, she thought, no broken wrist can possibly hurt as much as my heart does right now.

There was a brief pause. 'I'm staying, Gianna, whether you want me or not.'

She shrugged. 'Suit yourself.'

She heard the rocking chair creak as he sat down. Then there was no sound. She began to imagine she could hear the building breathing.

The silence was more than she could bear. She sat up a few minutes later, and said, 'What I meant was, you don't even have to stay in town, Blake.'

He gave her a long, speculative look. 'Why are you so anxious to get rid of me, Gianna?'

She laughed shakily. 'Because it's so very apparent that you'd have a better time with Meghan than here taking care of me.'

'How generous of you! And what makes you so sure I was going with Meghan?'

'Really, Blake, it was fairly obvious. You did say you wanted me to do the talk show——'

'I meant the two of us, Gianna.'

Stupid, she told herself, that such a simple little phrase could bring tears to her eyes. *The two of us*, he said, as if they ever could be partners again, in any real sense of the word!

'But the last couple of weeks,' he went on, 'you've been so busy sniping at me that you've had no time to listen.'

It stung her pride, all the more so because it was true. She struck back blindly. 'And you haven't even been there. Now, all of a sudden, it takes both of us to do this stupid show. What's the matter, Blake? Don't you trust me?'

'We certainly don't seem to be seeing eye to eye on much of anything these days——'

'Then why do you want me there at all? Maybe we shouldn't be trying to run a business together any more, Blake! Is that what you're really saying? Maybe we should just break up the partnership!'

The words hung in the air. Then Blake said heavily, 'Perhaps we should, Gianna.'

There was a long silence. She was horrified at the echo of the words she had said. Westway was all they had left, the only thing that held them together. Without it, she might never see him again.

I can't bear that, she thought. However painful it is to see him, it would be worse to be without him. And it would be worst of all to see him occasionally, and pretend there were no painful memories.

'What happened to us, Blake?' It was an agonised whisper. 'We were friends, until Meghan came along——'

'It wasn't Meghan's fault,' he said gruffly.

Gianna sighed. 'You're right,' she admitted. 'It was me.' Any woman who had threatened her peace of mind as Meghan had would have caused the same reaction, she knew. Meghan had merely been more beautiful than most, more glamorous, more appealing—more threatening.

'Why?' he asked. She hardly recognised his voice. The warmth, the laughter, was gone. 'That's what I don't understand, Gianna. Why did you pull away from me? You were never that way before. You were always warm, and full of laughter, and ready to have fun. Those were the things I loved about you——'

Loved? The word seemed to strike deep into Gianna's heart. As a friend, she told herself. He means he loved me as a friend. 'At any rate,' she said, trying to keep her voice calm, 'this scarcely matters now. I can't think Meghan would be very pleased at you having a woman for a best friend.'

'And why,' he said softly, 'do you think Meghan would have anything to say about it?'

She blinked. 'You are going to marry her, aren't you?'

'I haven't asked her.'

'Why not? It's obvious from looking at you that you're head over heels. And she thinks the world of you—any woman would. She'd have to be crazy to turn you down——' She choked to a halt, her throat tight.

Blake was staring at her, as if he'd never quite seen her before. 'Why do you say that?' he said, very softly. 'You did—turn me down, that is.'

Gianna stared at him, mouth open.

'There must be something wrong with my technique,' he speculated. There was a note in his voice that she had never heard before. 'I've proposed to you half a dozen times——'

'This isn't funny, Blake.'

'Obviously I haven't hit on quite the right note.' He looked thoughtful for a moment, then snapped his fingers. 'I've got it! Marry me, Gianna, and you'll never have to use the phone to call me in the middle of the night when you have a great idea——'

The mere thought of him, beside her in her big brass bed, making love to her, teasing her, holding her, sent waves of painful desire through her body. Enough, she thought grimly. I'm going to end this torture. 'What would you do if I said yes?'

'Is that your answer?'

'I haven't answered yet. I simply asked what you would do.'

He picked up the telephone and dragged the long cord across the carpet so he could set the instrument on the coffee table. Without a word, he dialled a number.

Gianna stood in the centre of the room, one hand on her hip. The broken wrist, even with the support of the sling, was beginning to throb. She tried to ignore it. 'Who are you calling?' she asked.

Blake ignored her and said, 'Hello, Mom. I thought you'd like to know that I just proposed to Gianna and she said——' He looked up enquiringly.

'Very funny,' muttered Gianna. 'I suppose you're talking to the time-and-temperature recording.' She reached for the telephone. Blake held it out of her reach, and she finally made a grab and snatched it from his hand. 'You have a juvenile sense of humour, you know,' she went on.

'Well, Blake?' said an anxious feminine voice in her ear. 'What did she say?'

'Gwen?' Gianna gasped. The receiver slipped from her nerveless hand, and she looked up at Blake. 'My God, you're serious!' she breathed.

'I'll call you later, Mom,' said Blake and put the telephone down ruthlessly.

'You're actually serious!' Gianna's breath was coming in harsh spurts. 'But you told me one night that you'd die of shock if I said yes—— You couldn't mean it. I've never heard anything so ridiculous!'

Blake sighed, and suddenly looked twice his age. 'You're right,' he said heavily. 'I suppose it is ridiculous, for me to think for even an instant that you might care——' He paced across the room, then turned from the darkness of the window and said, 'But dammit, Gianna, it doesn't seem ridiculous to me? Why shouldn't we get married? We like the same things, the same people. We get along well. We——'

Not a word about loving her. Well, she asked herself, what had she expected? 'Don't forget we could save a fortune,' she said drily.

He stood up. 'Don't laugh at me, Gianna,' he said. 'Because, you see, it's no joke to me. I've tried to make it one, to remind myself that I had no reason to believe you'd ever feel the same way I did. I've waited, and hoped, and tried to make you see how much I cared for you.'

'Blake?' she whispered. She reached out, afraid to believe she was hearing this.

'Oh, what's the point in saying all this?' He turned away. 'I was only tormenting myself. It should have been apparent to any man with eyes that you didn't give a darn about me. No woman tries to find dates for a man she might want for herself.'

Sometimes she does, Gianna thought, remembering Cluny. She hadn't known she wanted him, then. It hurt her to hear the savage note in his voice, the hint of despair. And yet it was impossible to believe that this was really happening!

'I even tried to convince myself, when you brought Meghan into the picture, that it was fate,' Blake went on.

'I told myself that any man who passed up a chance at Meghan was a fool, especially when the woman he thought he wanted didn't give a damn about him. Well, I'm here to tell you, my dear, that I'm a fool.'

Gianna swallowed hard. 'You mean——'

'I mean I'd spent only about three and a half minutes alone with Meghan before I discovered that it didn't make any difference who she was. I was head over heels and permanently in love with you.'

Gianna was having a little trouble breathing. Her wrist itched under the cast. She tried to scratch it, and succeeded only in snagging a fingernail against a rough edge on the plaster. She didn't even notice. Her head was swimming with the sudden effect of Blake's announcement.

'You kissed her,' she said uncertainly. 'I saw you—on New Year's Eve, and again today——'

'Of course I did. I knew you were there. I hoped it would make you think a little——' He slammed one fist into his other hand, and turned away with a muttered curse. 'Well, that's the story. I suppose only an idiot would let himself believe what I did. Even this morning—some of the things you said—I thought it might mean that you were actually jealous. I thought once Meghan was out of the way, we could sort it all out. But then you ran from me——'

Meghan means nothing to him, she thought. It's me he loves! She realised abruptly that he was walking towards the door. She tried to speak, and her voice caught in her throat. I have to stop him, she thought, in sudden panic. I can't let him go now! Blake's hand was on the knob when she found her voice.

'I was so jealous of Meghan,' she said clearly, 'that I wanted to scratch out those glorious green eyes every time I looked at her.'

He turned to face her. There was shock on his face, as if he wanted to believe her but couldn't force himself to do so. Then, as she moved across the room and let her hand brush his cheek, he reached for her, hesitantly, as if she might vanish from his grasp.

'I didn't know at first why it bothered me so much,' she confessed. 'I just knew it was driving me crazy to see you with her.'

His hands rested on her shoulders. 'Then all the boring hours I spent with her weren't wasted after all?'

Gianna let herself be drawn close. How warm he was, she thought vaguely, and how neatly the contours of her body fitted against his. But there was still one thing she had to get clear. Boring?' she asked. 'You never looked bored.'

He looked down at her, one eyebrow raised.

'I was watching,' she admitted in a whisper.

'Meghan,' he said with heartfelt relief, 'doesn't have a brain in her head. Curtis has taught her to be quiet, aloof and distant because if she opens her mouth, it immediately becomes obvious that she's a beautiful idiot.'

The touch of his hands sent fire leaping through Gianna's veins. She raised her head, and the brilliance of his eyes stopped the breath in her throat. His mouth was gently demanding, and she responded with an abandon that would have shocked her had she been able to feel anything but the glory of their shared passion. It was a long time before she could breathe again, and longer until she could speak.

'You scared me half to death on Christmas Eve,' she said thickly.

Blake kissed her, softly and gently. 'You were so beautiful, there in the firelight,' he said.

'Now I know you meant it when you said you love me,' she interrupted with an unsteady smile. 'Any man who spends an evening with Meghan and then tells me I'm beautiful has got to be in love!'

He held her a fraction of an inch away from him. 'Can

you be serious, please? I'm practising a seduction technique here.'

'Oh, by all means practise.' He sat down and pulled her on to his lap. She settled herself even closer against him.

'About Christmas Eve,' he murmured. 'It was the first Christmas we'd spent together in years. And I've been patient so long, Gianna——'

'How long?' She hardly knew she had asked. His hands were gently stroking her body, until every cell was on fire.

'Longer than I want to think about. Believe me, I didn't plan to fall in love with you. It was all so nice just the way it was.'

She nodded. She knew exactly how he had felt.

'I tried to talk myself out of it. But there was no making it go away. And that night—well, I just couldn't be patient any longer, Gianna. When you kissed me, it was like the answer to all my dreams—and then my fantasy blew up in my face.'

'I scared myself, I think,' she said meditatively. 'I expected it to be just a friendly kiss, and when it wasn't, I panicked.'

'And I thought you'd found me so repulsive that you'd never give me another chance to get near you.'

She shook her head, definitely. 'No, never that, Blake.'

'I'm glad,' he murmured.

'You didn't really answer my question,' she reminded him. 'How long have you known?'

'It started about the time you moved in here. I kept finding myself thinking about how practical it would be, and that some day we really ought to think about getting married.'

'How flattering!'

'You must admit it makes sense,' he argued. 'But then I found myself getting jealous of every man you told me about, and when I tried to figure out why, I came up against a stone wall—I realised I'd fallen in love with you. I tried to convince myself at the time that I was crazy.'

'What a charming thing to tell me!' Gianna said ruefully.

'You were so damned pleased to be my friend, you see, and I was afraid, if I said or did anything to upset that, I'd lose you altogether. I was stuck. No matter what I did, you treated me like a big brother, and I was afraid that if I pushed you, you'd back away entirely. So I waited, and hoped that some day you'd wake up and realise you wanted more than my friendship. When you did, I intended to be there waiting.'

'No matter how long it took?'

He sighed. 'No matter. But I didn't expect it to take as long as it did. So when Meghan came alone—I was ready to do anything I could to give you a push.'

'I'd have liked to push you both into the river!'

Blake grinned down at her, and her heart turned over. 'Good,' he said. 'You still haven't given me an answer. I'm tired of walking a line, my dear. What's it going to be?'

'Let's see,' she murmured. 'What are my choices again?'

He stood up suddenly, dumping her off his lap on to the floor. 'Let me know whenever you decide, so I can end my mother's suspense.'

Gianna scrambled to her feet. 'I'm amazed she hasn't called back.'

'She's probably still on the phone to Florida.'

'Without a doubt.' It didn't bother her any more.

'You still haven't said yes or no, Gianna,' Blake reminded her.

She smiled up at him. 'Yes, of course. I do love you, Blake. I think I always have, but I wasn't smart enough to know it.'

He took a deep breath. 'And I wasted all that time?'

'Tell your mother she's a genius,' Gianna recommended. 'And speaking of telephone calls, I suppose I'd better call Mr Elliot. I told him I'd get back to him this afternoon. I hope he's still in the office.'

'Elliot?' Blake asked warily.

'Yes. By the way, how do you feel about buying a house?'

He groaned. 'Dripping taps, pavements to shovel, and bats!'

'It's close to work,' she pointed out.

'That's true.'

'Besides, think about the pride of ownership. It does need all new wallpaper, though.'

'Oh, I thought the butterflies were all right.'

'How do you know which house I'm talking about?' She looked up at him. 'Have you been talking to my mother?'

'No. I've been talking to Elliot.'

'Really?'

'Yes. It's yet another symptom of my insanity—the fact that I almost bought the house you wanted, just so I'd be prepared in case you eventually decided to marry me.'

'Oh.' Gianna thought that one over, and smiled. 'If you really think it's insane, we don't have to buy the house,' she pointed out. 'We could just redecorate your apartment.'

'Let's buy the house.'

'You don't have to do it to please me, if you don't like the idea. It's a lot of money.'

'They'll take less. And watch it, Gianna. If you start getting too agreeable, you'll begin to sound like Meghan.'

'Blake,' she asked sweetly, 'are you certain you wouldn't rather marry Meghan? She wouldn't try to bully you.'

'Yes, she would. She's sweetness and light on the surface, and hard underneath. She was trying to make me give up coffee for good!'

'The only thing I'll make you swear off is models.'

Gianna punctuated the order with a kiss.

'Gladly.' Then Blake added, 'Besides, we'll need a house. There isn't enough room here to raise kids.'

'Oh,' she said softly, 'I hadn't thought of that.'

'We don't have to, of course—but our parents——'

'Would love to be grandparents,' Gianna agreed. 'By the way, how are you at hanging wallpaper?'

'Terrible,' he said promptly.

'Well, I dare say I can learn.'

'Do me a favour,' said Blake, 'and don't try.'

'But it looks so easy.'

'Until you find yourself wrapped in a double roll of the stuff,' he agreed, 'and I have to come and rescue you.'

'Well, I don't suppose it comes with a guarantee.'

'Nothing does, love.' He put his arms around her. 'Except you, of course.'

She pulled away a fraction of an inch and looked up enquiringly. 'And just what does that mean?'

'It means, Gianna, that anyone with enough nerve to marry you will find that life is never dull.' He kissed her, slowly and lingeringly. 'And that, my love, is just the way I like it.'

Harlequin
American Romance™
Harlequin celebrates the American woman...

...by offering you romance stories written about American women, by American women for American women. This series offers you contemporary romances uniquely North American in flavor and appeal.

◆

Harlequin Temptation™
Passionate stories for today's woman

An exciting series of sensual, mature stories of love...dilemmas, choices, resolutions... all contemporary issues dealt with in a true-to-life fashion by some of your favorite authors.

◆

Harlequin Intrigue™
Because romance can be quite an adventure

Harlequin Intrigue, an innovative series that blends the romance you expect... with the unexpected. Each story has an added element of intrigue that provides a new twist to the Harlequin tradition of romance excellence.

◆

Harlequin Books™

PROD-A-2

You'll flip . . . your pages won't!
Read paperbacks *hands-free* with

Book Mate · I

The perfect "mate" for all your romance paperbacks

Traveling • Vacationing • At Work • In Bed • Studying
• Cooking • Eating

Perfect size for
all standard
paperbacks,
this wonderful
invention
makes reading
a pure pleasure!
Ingenious
design holds
paperback
books OPEN
and FLAT so
even wind can't
ruffle pages —
leaves your
hands free to do
other things.
Reinforced,
wipe-clean vinyl-
covered holder flexes to let you
turn pages without undoing the
strap . . . supports paperbacks so
well, they have the strength of
hardcovers!

Pages turn WITHOUT
opening the strap.

SEE-THROUGH STRAP

Reinforced back stays flat.

Built in bookmark.

BOOK MARK

BACK COVER
HOLDING STRIP

10" x 7¼", opened.
Snaps closed for easy carrying, too.

Available now. Send your name, address, and zip code, along with a check or
money order for just $5.95 + .75¢ for postage & handling (for a total of $6.70)
payable to Reader Service.

> Reader Service
> Bookmate Offer
> 901 Fuhrmann Blvd.
> P.O. Box 1396
> Buffalo, N.Y. 14269-1396

Offer not available in Canada
*New York and Iowa residents add appropriate sales tax.

BM-G